Dance By Midnight

The Grimoire Chronicles
Book One

CALDWELLPRESS.COM

Published by Caldwell Press

Thank you for purchasing and reading Dance By Midnight. It would be greatly appreciated if you could take a moment and leave an honest review of this book within the guidelines of your favorite retailer.

QUALITY CONTROL: If you find typos or formatting problems, please contact ph8dra@comcast.net so they may be corrected.

If you want to be notified when Phaedra's next novel is released and get free stories and occasional other goodies, please sign up for her mailing list at her website, phaedraweldon dot com.

Your email address will never be shared and you can unsubscribe at any time.

As always for my father, his memory, and the legacy he left behind.
To my mother, my family, and to my daughter.
And finally to a fellow fan of Icehouse, Darren McKinty, who became the inspiration for the character.

"A lady, with whom I was riding in the forest, said to me, that the woods always seemed to her to wait, as if the genii who inhabit them suspended their deeds until the wayfarer has passed onward: a thought which poetry has celebrated in the dance of the fairies, which breaks off on the approach of human feet."

-Ralph Waldo Emerson

THE GiRL iN THE BOOTS

Most people have childhood memories. I don't. And I had come to accept that my childhood was filled with mystery. I even thought that was cool for a while, back when I couldn't get enough of super heroes. Thought of myself as having an origin story—only I didn't know what the story was.

So at the age of twenty-four, I decided to look for my past in hopes it would explain my present. Explain my ability to see ghosts. Explain how I could live with a magic book bound to my soul.

That journey started with a spell that promised to restore my memories of my beginning. But like all spells, it needed ingredients. One of the most poignant of those ingredients is the graveyard dust of my forefathers. The only forefather I knew of was my grandfather, buried in Savannah, Georgia.

That brings me to where I am now. Laurel Grove Cemetery, just after midnight. It was the beginning of February and cold. I'm not a fan of graveyards, and though I was relieved I didn't have to visit Bonaventure Cemetery with its ancient mausoleums and massive tombstones, I was still creeped out. Laurel had a few mausoleums here and there, and of course one of them was near where I had to be. I held my phone up, the flashlight app on, and clumsily made my way down the row to my family plot where my grandfather, Torbin A. McConnell, was buried.

I smelled water and all things green as a breeze sifted through the trees. My light shined down on the marble slab that keep the dead firmly in the ground, and I wondered what part of the grave constituted graveyard dust?

Ten seconds later, I found myself trying to breathe as an Angel strangled the 'effing shit out of me.

She didn't look like any Angel found in a book or a movie or on TV. She wasn't all gracious and golden and glowing with love and light either. Gabriel was tall, lithe and scary as hell. She reminded me of Switch from *The Matrix*, wearing white boots, white vinyl pants, white crop top and a long white leather trench coat. The entire scary picture was topped off by a head full of spiky white hair. She had me off the ground. My feet dangled beneath me as she pressed my back against the icy marble of a mausoleum wall. I had my best death grip on her wrists and tried with much enthusiasm, but little success, to pull her off of me.

She didn't start her attack with the strangle dance. In fact, she surprised me with a right cross as she materialized to my left from thin air. I saw stars, kicked at her as she dove at me again and tried to run. That's when something very solid and very painful nailed the back of my legs. I literally flipped in the air as I ran and landed on my ass. That's when she grabbed my neck, dragged me to that mausoleum and pushed me up against the side of it and started yelling.

"Answer me, Guardian—what are you looking for in a graveyard at midnight? Dust perhaps? Or maybe even a bone or two? Did something whisper to you from that damned book in your soul?"

See? A book in my soul. Unfortunately it's a book a lot of different… creatures…want.

I suspected Gabriel wasn't going to kill me. She'd hounded me since the book and I were joined and she hadn't ended me yet. Given her power she could at any time. I suspected her reluctance had something to do with the book itself. I'd heard nothing but stories of how powerful it was since learning it was there. Secretly, I think she's afraid of it.

I closed my eyes and focused on the Grimoire. That's what they all called the book. Someone who knows a great deal about the book told me my best defense was to learn to use the book. They always said that desperate times usually drove us toward desperate measures. Well—her exact words were "when the student is ready, the teacher will come." I took that to mean the person to teach me how to use the book's magic would show up just before something killed me.

My name's Dags McConnell. First name's really Darren. I have no idea where the nickname Dags came from. I'm around 5'7, with dark brown hair and gray eyes. I love long walks on the beach and apparently having my ass kicked.

I tried to answer her, I *really* did. My face grew warm and spots did a hula in front of my eyes. I lost feeling in my hands and feet and not because of the temperature. I could see my breath in the cold…that is…if I could breathe.

"I'm right, aren't I? You're using the Grimoire to find a way to get rid of me. Maybe I should lock you away, keep you close by until you finally die and then take—"

I heard the dog about a beat after she did, barking and growling nearby. Gabriel turned her frighteningly beautiful face away and peered into the darkness. "It…it *can't* be…"

A light appeared about eye level with me in the distance. It started out as a pinpoint but quickly grew in size and I realized about the same time she did that it was coming right at us.

Gabriel released me just before whatever it was struck the mausoleum. Luckily, gravity brought me under it and I collapsed on all fours, hacking and coughing as I struggled to bring air into my lungs. My neck hurt, but my head hurt worse. When I looked up and back at the mausoleum's side in the moonlight, I saw scorch marks in the shape of a large pentagram.

That's when a dog—no, a *wolf*—stepped out of the surrounding darkness and padded up beside me. It nudged my shoulder and gently pushed me to the left of the mausoleum wall. I could have sworn it was trying to herd me away from the mausoleum. I kept my cool—*barely*—since I'd never been nose to nose with a large gray wolf before.

Gabriel's white clothing made her a moving target in the twilight. The nearly full moon illuminated everything about her, screaming *Pick me! Pick me!* She practically glowed. "Come out. I can sense your power, Witch."

Witch?

No no no no…not another Witch.

With that knowledge, it was time to exit stage left. I ventured forth slowly—because I was in some serious physical pain—and turned in the direction Gabriel wasn't facing with the visualization of getting to my car and getting the hell out of there. I'd dropped my phone somewhere but wasn't going to risk my life to find it.

Only…the wolf was in my way. If I tried to move to either side of it, it growled and showed teeth. So I remained on my ass, hidden in the shadow of the mausoleum, guarded by a gray wolf. I didn't think my life could get any weirder.

"You gotta be kiddin' me." The voice had a slight southern lilt and belonged to a young woman. "What in the hell brings an Angel into a cemetery at midnight?"

She appeared out of the darkness and stood several feet away from Gabriel. "You know you're not supposed to be here, Cherubim. And you, of all of the Ethereals, know this is a serious breech of protocol. So, I'm going to have to ask you to leave."

I gave her points for spunk. Her outfit added to that spunk. Tight jeans moved smoothly into some serious cowboy boots. A short-sleeved white button-down hung untucked beneath an oversized black vest that would probably look more at home in a men's three-piece suit.

Dark hair hung long over her shoulders. What I could see of her face in the twilight was beautiful.

Gabriel scowled. "Who the fuck are you?"

"I'm your worst nightmare." Her expression remained serious for about two beats before she erupted in laughter and waved her hand dismissively. "I've always wanted to say that!"

"This is not a game, little Witch. You are no match for me. Now if you care to survive and not become a Power just to entertain me, then I suggest you leave. *Now.*"

A Power was an Ethereal's slave, a host for Angelic essence created and controlled by a Virtue. Powers inhabited dead bodies and did their maker's bidding. I guess Cherubims, as well as Virtues, could make them? I didn't like the idea of her doing that to the girl in the boots. But how was I going to help when I had such limited resources? Not to mention I was starting to feel a *lot* of pain.

"Sorry, *sweetie*, but I'm not in the mood. See I've got business out here myself, and I don't need an Angel tainting the place or torturing poor little kids."

Little kids?

"What the hell are you? Just stupid?" Gabriel sounded as confused as she did angry. This girl interrupted her play-date with me.

The girl in the boots put her hands on her hips. "I'm a child of the God Mother. And it's my job to keep your kind out of where it doesn't belong."

Gabriel spat at her. "You don't have the power."

"Lady Darksome…." the girl in the boots sighed as she lowered her hands. "Angels really are arrogant. Now…I can't stand here and chitchat. It's time for you to go back to where you came." She raised her arms again; only this time she moved them in opposite directions, the right arm making a right-handed arc, the left making a left-handed arc. The movement created bright lines in the air in front of her, forming a symbol that remained suspended in brilliant blue and white light. "I am a Child of the Wandering Wide. I call upon the gates of future and past and cast you back into the world you hold so dear," she held out her hands. *"So mote it be!"*

I didn't really expect anything to happen. I mean—Gabriel was a Cherubim and they're like the upper crust of the First Choir, or we can call it the *In Crowd*. Hell, I'd seen several people go up against Angels and get their asses handed to them in seconds. Including mine. So I was a bit upset this girl in the boots was about to have what I could only assume was a nice little butt treated in the same way.

Only…that's not what happened.

Gabriel looked confused, especially as the girl in the boots started her incantation (which she said *really* fast). I thought Gabriel would counter the spell or block it. But even after Boots released it, which I figured the "so mote it be!" was for, I didn't see anything. No light show, no blinding auras, no sparks.

It took a few seconds before I realized Gabriel was gone. Not even a pop sound. Just…there one minute, gone the next.

I relaxed back against the mausoleum wall. The cold replaced the air around me and I shivered. My toes were already goners 'cause I couldn't feel them. That's when I realized Gabriel had yanked me right out of my shoes.

The girl smacked her hands together as if getting the dirt off and then came toward me. I held up my hand as the wolf bounded to her and to my shock and horror, pounced on her. Only it wasn't in a *grrrr I'm gonna eat you* way. It was more in a fun, loving, *I wanna be your bed buddy* way.

Apparently they knew each other.

She snapped her fingers and a light appeared over her hand. It hovered for a second before ascending above us to stop a few feet over our heads. The light was pretty bright, but the height diffused the glow—like having a private sun. When I looked into it, I thought I saw a lizard. She squatted with her knees against her chest and leaned in close. "Wow…she did a number on you. You're going to have a black eye…and a black cheek. Oh, and your jaw is looking a bit bad too. Can you walk?"

I nodded to her, mesmerized by her face. She was prettier up close, or was it the twilight that did it? Blue eyes clothed in darker makeup. She was almost goth, but not quite. Which was kinda hot.

To prove to her I could move and not be the helpless dude, I started to get up. The stars that filled my vision robbed me of my dignity as I fell back against the side of the mausoleum, nauseated. Oh god…I was going to lose my cookies in front of a good-looking woman.

"Okay, we'll call that a no." She reached out to my head and where she touched, it hurt. I winced. "Sorry. Looks like she might have rammed your head into that marble. Concussion…probably why you look like hammered shit. Is your mom nearby? Got a cell we can call her on?"

I cleared my throat. "Not a kid. Twenty-six."

Her eyes widened. "Wow…I need more light, cause you look really young. And you…." she said as she sat back, staring at me.

I was light headed and the pounding between my ears intensified. My palms itched (no jokes, please) and felt warm, like holding them over an open fire.

"What…what the hell *are* you?" She held up her hand and a large, complicated pentagram appeared between us. It spun like a combination lock as she concentrated on it. To the right, then the left, then back to the right.

My eyelids felt like lead. I looked at her through slits. Yeah, I was going to pass out. I was gonna faint in front of this hot chick and she was going to bash my head in with her kick ass boots. "Tourist," I managed to say.

She spoke as she watched the pentagram. "Dude…you're not just some tourist. Tourists don't glow the way you're—" her eyes widened as she dismissed the huge star, got on her feet and came close again. "Oh man…so that's why that Angel was here messing where she shouldn't be." She gave me a half smile. Her hair was long and brushed over her arms. "My *dex* says you're a child of the God Mother!"

Yippie?

A FACE FOR SORE EYES

I sort of jolted awake. My arms and knees came up as I tried to get my balance. Something wet and cold slipped off of my face. I didn't know where I was, when I was, how I was—

"Hey, relax. Nothing's getting through to this place, 'kay? Just take a few deep breaths. You took a good ding to the head—but if I remember right—yours is a commodity harder than granite."

I *knew* that voice. The sound of it brought back a boatload of images. A red headed woman smiling, a small blonde 'tweener, a window full of twinkling crystals—

When I opened my eyes, I zeroed in on a face I hadn't seen in years. "Mike? Mike Ross?"

He grinned down at me. It *was* him. A friend I'd met and chummed around with in Roswell, Georgia. We'd hit it off and shared a few beers, did a bit of ghost hunting, and even managed to diffuse a cursed object. "You recognize me. I figure that's a good thing, means your head's okay. Nothing scrambled."

Oh he didn't know the half of it. "Mike…it so good to see a familiar face." My smile turned upside down. "What're you doing in Savannah?" I tried to sit up again. "We're still in Savannah, right?"

He put a hand on my shoulder again and gave it a gentle push so I would lie back down. "Yeah, we're still here. We're at my place in

Madison Square. Old town. Sam's got the townhouse warded like Fort Knox so like I said, no Angel's getting to you."

"Sam?"

"Samantha. She said an Angel beat you up in the graveyard. Now, I remember a lot of things from back in Roswell, but I never figured you'd go picking fights with Angels."

The things he said weren't congruent with the things I remembered. "You…*know* about the Angels?"

"I know about the worlds, if that's what you're asking. Still learning the hierarchy. Five worlds. Remember you used to tell me that? Physical, Mental, Astral, Ethereal and Abysmal." He grinned again. Mike had grown a scraggly beard and his hair was longer now, over his ears. "Been over two years since I saw you. You disappeared from the radar," Mike pursed his lips as he twisted his head toward his right shoulder. "You look different, Dags. I almost didn't recognize you."

"Yeah well, we all change as we grow." I was in a bed, my shirt missing—in fact everything was missing!—in what looked like a spare bedroom. I figured that because a few cardboard boxes were stacked in the farthest corner, blinds covered the windows, and a set of golf clubs was propped up by a closet door. Sticking out of the closet was a weight bench and accessories. I poked at his upper arm. It felt like steel under his skin. "You've changed too. You look…bigger." I wasn't joking. Mike was wearing a "wife beater" t-shirt and he looked like a body builder.

"I keep in shape more now than I did." He stood and that's when I saw he'd been sitting on what looked like a bar stool. "It's been a rough year. Got into some scrapes now and then. But you look…where the hell have you been?"

I pushed myself up onto my elbows and then made it to a sitting position with my legs off the bed. I also made sure the sheets kept my privates private. "A lot's happened, Mike, since we saw each other. A fucking hell of a lot."

"Sam called you a God Mother's child. A Guardian."

"Yeah."

"What does that mean?"

"I have no idea."

"That's 'effed up, Dags. So…you got the tattoos removed," he pointed to my hand.

I looked at the palm. "You knew about the tattoos?"

"Well yeah. Stella called and told me what you did, wanted me to come and blast your ass for letting some complete stranger brand you. Don't you remember?"

Stella Rosenberg. She'd been my landlady in Atlanta…among other things.

"Someone branded him?" Sam came to the door then, a mug in her hand. She looked different. Her hair was pulled back from her face on the sides and the makeup was toned down. "Someone should teach him how to fight, or at least defend himself." She handed the mug to me. "It's hot, so grab the handle."

I did and she was right, it was hot. I held it under my nose. It smelled like peppermint and honey. "What is it?"

"My version of a hot toddy. It'll put some color back in those cheeks."

Mike nodded to her. "Sam's a great healer, among other things."

"I needed a healer?"

"You remember what the Angel did?"

I sipped the toddy. It was spicy and sweet. I liked it. "I remember it hurt."

"She broke your head, Mr. McConnell."

"Just call me Dags."

"That's a funny name."

"So's Sam. Rhymes with Spam."

She looked at Mike. "I say we roast him. I can sell his clothing and the SUV."

I glared at her but didn't comment. I wanted more of the hot toddy. My headache was gone but I still felt woozy.

"What were you doing in Laurel Cemetery?" Mike asked.

That question brought a sigh to the surface. "Remember my mysterious past?"

"Yeah. Mother died in a fire. You were found in a tree."

Sam looked from Mike to me. "Found in a tree?"

"Yeah. My dad said I ran from the house the day of the fire and disappeared. Took them a few days to find me because I was actually sleeping inside of an old tree husk. They had to pry me out. I woke up screaming and then went back to sleep for a long time. I don't have any memory of that time and I didn't show any signs of exposure to being outside," I shrugged. "I've never been able to explain it. So I went looking for a way to open my memories and found a spell—but one of the ingredients is the graveyard dust of my forefathers."

"You sure you don't mean graveyard dirt?" Sam asked.

"Could be?"

"Dags, you have to know which one. Dust is the dust from the bones. You have to go inside the grave to get it off the body. Dirt is the dirt inside the grave, not inside the coffin. Both are used for hoodoo, not Witch magic. Dirt's used to commune with the spirits."

"And dust?"

"Dark stuff. You get this spell from a hoodoo?"

"I…don't know. I got it from a woman in Atlanta."

"Ah. Could be then. So, that's when the Angel showed up? Didn't get the dirt?"

"No."

"We can try again. I'll look at the spell later and see if I can help. So," she leaned towards me. "Branded?"

I repeated what Mike and I'd already talked about before she came in. "And yeah, it was a stupid thing to do. But like I told him, I didn't remember having it done. It was this Ceremonial Magic group in Atlanta. I went to one of their rituals and the dude in charge said it was for purification for me and three others because we were going to represent the four corners—"

"Quarters. Circles don't have corners. Basic geometry," Sam smiled.

I glared. "*Quarters.* I was designated Air and I drank something in a chalice—"

"You didn't ask what it was?"

"No."

"And you drank it?"

"Yeah."

"You knew these people?"

I set the mug on a nightstand by the bed. "Look, I already admitted it was a stupid thing to do because when I woke up my palms were tattooed."

She reached out and took my wrist. Her fingers were thin and her nails buffed.

"He had them removed and doesn't remember it," Mike said.

"Oh...they're not removed. They're still there." She pulled my hand flat, pulling my fingers back to a point where I winced and tried to pull it away. "The marks are under the skin. Looks like...something integrated the...." she stopped and looked at me. "*Who* did this?"

"I don't know the tattoo artist's name—"

"Uh uh. I'm asking who authorized this? Where did this symbol come from? Who was the leader of this idiotic group?" Witches and Magicians didn't much care for one another. I wasn't sure why.

I sighed, feeling as embarrassed now as I'd been then about my own stupidity. "Well the guy that authorized this was named Allard Bonville, but he—"

Sam moved faster than I expected. Not that I expected any movement. Before I could protest she had the hand and wrist she'd been examining wrenched up behind my back and I found myself kissing the floor. She sat on my bare ass and I swore I was going to get carpet burns on places I did *not* want carpet burns! "You're Cruorem!"

I cringed. Sometimes we just do stupid shit in our lives that follows us no matter where we go. I wanted to protest that I wasn't a member, and that as far as I knew, Bonville was no longer a threat. But that was just impossible because she had my face crushed into the carpet.

Embarrassment was also a key player for me at that moment. Twice in less than twenty-four hours two women had taken me down. I never thought of myself as a helpless dude. But I was seriously starting to think I was losing bro points.

I heard the all too familiar click of a gun safety being removed from a gun. "Samantha—let him go or I swear, Witch or not, I'll fucking blow your head off. Dags is the only friend I have and he knew Teresa and helped me with Brendi. Let. Him. Go."

Several seconds ticked by before she let go of my arm and took her knee off of my back. Mike grabbed the sheet from the bed and helped me to my feet. He stepped between Sam and I, the gun still in his hand, as I covered up. Things seemed so surreal at that moment—as long as I'd known Mike, I'd never seen him with a gun. I didn't even know he knew how to use one. And…it was a really big gun.

Sam stood several feet away by the bedroom door. She looked ready to bolt. "Cruorem are worthless pieces of trash. They don't use magic for good—and Bonville is the worst of them. They dabble in Arcane Magic."

I peeked out from behind Mike. Did I mention Mike's taller than me? I come to the top of his shoulders. "Arcane?"

She shifted her gaze from Mike to me. "Magic from the Other Worlds. The dark worlds. Bad shit, Dags. Like the use of graveyard dust," Sam shook her head. "The Cruorem have a bad rep."

"Hey, choir here. I admit it was stupid of me, but I told you, I didn't choose to have the tattoos. I woke up and they were there."

"So why are they integrated? And why are they pulsing?"

I looked at my hand. "I don't see anything pulsing."

"It's not something you can see. I felt it. The symbols are portals. Did you know that?"

I kept looking at my hand. "Portals? Doorways? For…something to come through or something to get in?"

"They feel like a connection piece. Something like a conduit between you and something else."

Turning my hand front and back, I looked at her. "So something can come through them?"

Sam's shoulders relaxed. "Yeah. I don't think that was their original purpose. They're linked to that book bound to your soul."

I put my hand to my chest as Mike finally moved. He stepped forward and turned to face me. "Book bound to your soul?"

Now they were *both* looking at me. I held out my hands (yes, the sheet was secure). "Look, I admit having the book inside is a bit weird—"

"You think?" Mike said.

"—but a Witch put it there to save my life. Honest!"

Mike reset the safety on the gun and tucked it into the back of his jeans, which just seemed a bit crazy to me. He *carried* a gun, not just used it? He sat on the bed and faced me. "A Witch bound a book to your soul to save your life. Shit Dags, and I thought *I* had a bad year."

"Your year wasn't caused by brain-dead stupidity," Sam's tone wasn't as sharp as her words. "This book—it's the old Cruorem Grimoire, isn't it? That was the feel I got when I was healing you."

"I guess…." I hated the fact that the only thing I could do was shrug. "So much of the past year is as blurry as my childhood." I ran a hand through my hair. My head hurt again.

Mike waved dismissively at me. "I'm sorry. You've had a rough year and it's okay. You've always been there when I needed you and now I know why you disappeared."

I searched his face and found something I didn't like. I couldn't read minds—or maybe I could and forgot how. But I knew Mike well enough, remembered him, that I recognized pain when I saw it. "Mike…what happened? Did you call me and I wasn't there?"

His face told me everything, and nothing. When I'd first met Mike he was married, and then a few months later he was in the middle of a divorce and discussing the custody of his daughter. She'd been fourteen at the time. Brendi. I remembered her because he brought her into the bar where I worked and she always asked me to make her a Shirley Temple with extra cherries.

When Mike looked away, I knew Brendi was the reason he was here in Savannah. "What happened—"

"Teresa's dead," his voice was flat and he moved away to the window. I watched him, aware of Sam's eyes on me. "Remember how we came to the agreement? That Brendi would stay with me while Teresa chased her job?"

"Yeah..."

"Well, Teresa moved, ended up in Seattle. Brendi and I were happy. The store did pretty good for a while, but when the economy tanked and I found myself in a sort of financial strait, I called Teresa to see if she could help take care of Brendi till I got back on my feet. Teresa didn't answer my calls and she always had before. I really started worrying when Brendi's birthday came and went and Teresa didn't send anything, she didn't even visit, and before then she never missed our daughter's birthday."

I put my hand to the wall, my knees shaky. I already sort of knew what he was going to say and I didn't *want* to hear it.

"Seattle Police contacted me. They found Teresa's body in her home, ripped apart. Said it looked like some kind of animal had mauled her. I had to account for my whereabouts...." he looked at me. "Like I could ever do that to Teresa?"

"No."

"I didn't know how to tell Brendi. She was at school when I got the call. I'd put her in a private school—that's what I needed financial help with. So after I hung up with the police, I called the school to arrange to pick her up early. But they told me she wasn't there. She'd been counted absent," he looked down. "I dropped her off that morning, just like I always did. I walked inside, kissed her cheek, and watched her go into her room. There was no way she wasn't there."

"What did you do?"

"I raised holy hell is what I did. I stormed into that school—I was so angry, Darren. I terrified the teachers and students when I demanded to know where she was. I pointed at the kids that'd greeted her that morning and they lied to my face. They said they never saw me. So did the teacher. And my performance didn't ingratiate me with the police. They arrested me and then held me pending finding my daughter. When they coordinated with the Seattle PD, they decided I had something to do with Teresa's murder and my daughter's disappearance.

"I tried calling you but you didn't answer. I did get hold of Stella and she arranged bail."

"So what happened?"

"They ruled Teresa's death not a homicide because the ME there insisted she'd been killed by an animal, not a man. And too many witnesses placed me in Georgia at the time. They shipped her body back to South Carolina, but her parents wouldn't let me attend the funeral. They're the ones who want me behind bars. They say I killed Brendi, Darren. But I didn't."

All of my troubles, *magic-book-bound-to-soul* aside, seemed ridiculously petty. Mike had lost his ex-wife, someone he'd considered a close friend, as well as his daughter. I'd never married or even considered having kids...so I couldn't imagine the heartache he felt.

I thought Sam was going to approach Mike, but she walked past him to me and put a hand to my chest. Something fluttered inside and for a second Sam appeared to glow a bright blue white. It was the color of the symbols I'd seen her use in the cemetery.

"I'm here to help Mike find his daughter. She's still alive and her disappearance was orchestrated by someone from one of the Other Worlds."

"You...you think someone from one of the worlds killed Teresa and took Brendi?"

"I don't think. I *know*. My familiar can smell them. That's how I was able to find you in the cemetery. Through your smell."

"Your familiar?" I glanced at Mike.

"Grey. You met her in the graveyard."

The wolf?

I looked at Mike, hoping he could help me understand this. But he was still looking out the window. I made a decision at that moment. Whether it was out of guilt or the need to repay both of them for saving my bacon didn't matter. "I want to help, Mike. I wasn't there for you when it happened. So let me help you now."

Mike looked back at me. "Can you use a weapon?"

"No."

"Can you fight? Like hand to hand?"

"It's obvious he can't fight. Or he won't fight a girl," Sam's tone wasn't mean but her words stung.

"I—"

"Can you use this magic book? With your hands?"

"No, but I—"

Sam put a hand on my shoulder. It was warm and made my skin tingle. "It's okay Dags. You need to stay here and watch the house. Mike and I can find Brendi. Then after that, maybe I can teach you to fight."

I bit back a response as I watched her leave the room. I was a guest in Mike's house and Sam was obviously helping. It would be rude of me to start an argument no matter how much I wanted to.

When I looked at Mike, he turned back to the window and didn't say anything else. I couldn't help but feel I'd disappointed him.

FAERiES WiLL EAT YOUR FACE

Mike cooked while I explored. Sam took Grey out for a walk. I didn't realize I'd been asleep for so long. The last thing I remembered was being in the cemetery around two in the morning. Color me shocked when Mike offered to make hamburgers for *dinner*.

I looked around while he told me his version of last night. He'd been nearby in his Jeep waiting on a signal from Sam to let him know she'd found the Angel that Grey smelled. He'd been shocked when he'd walked up and saw me there, beaten and not moving.

"Look," Mike began from where he stood at the stove. He'd already made five patties of meat. How many burgers was he gonna eat? "I'm sorry. About Sam. She's the most determined woman I've ever met, and the first Witch I've ever met. She just wants to find Brendi, and thinks you'd be a liability."

I shoved my hands into my jeans. I didn't say anything. What was there to say? She was right. I was a guy with an all-powerful magic book inside of him and couldn't even physically defend himself against a woman. Not to seem sexist but…damn.

"Why was that Angel messing with you?"

I was at the sliding door, looking at the small but immaculate deck. The wood looked newly stained and the black iron banister shined under the southern sun. The rest of the yard, though small, reminded me of an English garden. Enclosed by a seven-foot fence draped in variegated ivy, a pond and fountain decorated the back half of the yard, with a semi-circle pattern mirrored on either side filled in with different plants. I was pretty sure the whole back yard bloomed in an array of colors in the spring.

"The Grimoire. Gabriel sees it, and me, as a threat and is waiting for me to die so she can make sure the Angels have it."

"Why doesn't she just kill you?"

"I don't know. I think she's afraid of it."

"So that's a thing."

I blinked and looked over at him. The townhouse was nice. The living room and dining area was wide open, and a marble countertop separated the kitchen and pantry. Two sets of stairs led to the second floor—one near the front door, the other beside the pantry door. The bedroom I'd slept in was on the second floor. Mike's was on the third. "Yeah. I guess it is. My power is an Angel is afraid of a book."

"Dags, soon as we get Brendi back, you can stay here and I can teach you how to fight, maybe join the local dojo? Show you how to fire a gun?" He flipped the last three burgers onto the pile he'd made on a platter and turned off the stove. When he turned to look at me, I noticed he'd aged more than two years. More than he should have. What he'd gone through had really taken it out of him. "So…is it like Sam said? It's a Book of Shadows?"

"I don't know if I'd call it that, but I think the principle's the same. I was told it was a compendium, a collection of spells dating back over a millennium."

"A millennium, huh. That's one old book."

"I don't think the physical book is that old, but the spells are. They were written down by a Demoness." I was surprised by Mike's apparent acceptance of things that when I was first learning about them, made me paranoid. "She was an Abysmal First Born. Do you know what that is?"

"A Vampire?"

Again, impressed. "So you know about their origin?"

"Yeah. They're called Revenants or something. They were born as demons and inhabit the bodies of humans and drink blood. But they're more of a symbiotic relationship, not one of master and slave. Doesn't mean I like it," he pursed his lips. "So the book bound to your soul was written by a Vamp. You know how Hollywood movie that sounds?"

"Yeah I do. But, it's the truth. She didn't write all of it. And she wrote it before she became a Revenant. There's centuries of spells in it."

He leaned forward on the counter and rested his elbows on the surface. "You think maybe—given what I've overheard you and Sam talk about—you're a part of the book now? Or the book is a part of you? I mean, if it's keeping you alive, is it possible you're keeping it alive?"

That was a damn good question—and just a bit too quantum physics for me. "I don't know Mike."

"Well, let's say you're part of each other," he shrugged. "Then shouldn't you be able to see what's in the book?"

"I don't know," I realized my tone was harsh so I softened it. "If there's a way to access it, I don't have it."

"So...you could be like Sam?"

"A Witch? She thinks I'm a Witch."

"Yeah, she mentioned that. You could do magic?"

"I don't know."

"You really don't know much, dude."

I wanted to just ignore the conversation. He was right. Why argue? But it still hurt.

Mike shrugged. "You know, there's a way you could help Sam and I?"

"How?" That sounded a little too desperate in my ears.

"You were always good with research, Dags. Remember? If I ever had a question about the weird things that came into my shop, I could always trust you to find out what it was."

Without knowing it, Mike struck to the very heart of what had been eating me since leaving Atlanta. I'd been in Savannah nearly a month, walked everywhere, probably taken every tourist train the city had, and when it came right down to it—I'd had no idea what to do. I had money. A lot of it. And I'd made sure it could only be accessed by me so the people I left couldn't take it back.

I put my hands on the back of a chair at the counter. "So…what is it you want me to research?"

He straightened up and fixed me with an intense stare. "Changelings."

* * *

My only knowledge of a Changeling came from old fairy tales I'd read as a child, back when I believed in things like fairies, elves, pixies, leprechauns and the Easter Bunny. Though, given the track my life jumped this past year—I don't think I'd be surprised if the Easter Bunny was real.

And ate children in egg salad.

Mike's computer was a newer model, the kind with the touch screen. And it was big. I sat in front of it for a few hours searching, using a few old access codes to information sites not readily available to the general public. Those places had the best info and I ended up meeting a few old friends in one of the secured chats. Seemed everyone thought I'd died.

>**Me**: Cy, I need info on Changelings.

>**IndigoCypher**: You wanna know about Faeries? You got a real death wish, bro? Stay the hell away from them. Nothing good comes from messing with them. All that shit in movies and TV about them being all pretty with wings and dust? Pure BS. Bad rumors to get us humans into their Cairns.

>**Me**: Cairns. I didn't think those were real.

>**IndigoCypher**: You said your mom used to dig them out of your yard, didn't you?

>**Me:** Yeah, but the gardeners and I always thought she was crazy.

>**IndigoCypher:** Nope. They're real. Cairns are their place between

us and where they come from. Truth is they feed on us, just like Vamps and other unworldly creatures of the night. They'll take you in with dust, man. You let that shit get on you and then they get in your heads. One of my sources told me he had one in his house. Got his dog, and the dog just stopped eating and starved to death. Looked like a mummy by the time the little fucker was done with it.

I sat back and mulled over what Cypher typed. I realized he and most of the others didn't know the truth of how things worked. They didn't know about the worlds, and the things that existed inside them. So, on the surface his information always read as a bit over the top. But deep down there was a bigger meaning. Sort of like myth with truth inside it, as a nugget of gold.

What I took from this was that everything I learned about Faeries as a kid was wrong. They weren't nice. And they weren't our friends. And they didn't die if we told them we didn't believe in them.

Or…did they?

Truth in the gooey center, after all.

>**Me**: How do Changelings fit in?

>**IndigoCypher**: Constructs. Faeries usually don't make a Changeling unless they want something they can't get normally. Like if their dust doesn't work? And that shit always works. So if it doesn't, what they're after is not human.

>**IndigoCypher**: Far as I know, it's made out of the stuff where they come from. Ether or essence or some word. They make it superficially real by taking a bit of their target and sticking it into the constructed thing. It's all a little cray-cray if you know what I mean.

>**Me**: And after they get what they want?

>**IndigoCypher**: Oh, that's when the thing goes apeshit and kills everything that knew its target. Once that's done, it just disappears.

>**Me**: And it won't die till it's done this?

>**IndigoCypher**: That's what I hear. Hey D, you don't have a Changeling after you, do you? Was that why you baked for a while?

>**Me**: No. At least I don't think so.

>**Me**: So how do you kill it?

>**IndigoCypher**: That's just it. You or I don't by ourselves. Two things can kill it—either one of those Watchers, those realm nazis and we all know they're dead, or a magic weapon. They can be burned I think, but you'd better cut off its head.

I ended the conversation with promises of logging in more and updating my own paranormal sites. Not that I had any real intention of doing that. For one...I'd forgotten most of my passwords.

Sam had stepped back into the townhouse at some point and I learned why Mike had made so many burgers. The wolf ate seven of them. No ketchup, please.

Mike and Sam were in the living room pouring over several big books on the coffee table. I idly wondered if the furniture was Mike's or if it came with the townhouse. Looked like something out of an IKEA catalogue. But the sight of the books reminded me of something.

"Where's my car?"

Mike looked up. "I drove it back. It was the easiest way to get you here. It's out front. Key's by the door."

I found the keys in a glass bowl and bounded outside—and stopped. I guess it hadn't dawned on me that Mike's townhouse was actually in one of Savannah's infamous squares. Madison Square, to be exact, which rested behind the DeSoto Hilton. Mike's townhouse was on the same street that backed up the hotel. I walked carefully down the iron staircase and spotted my car to the right. After rummaging around in the back and grabbing two bags—items I never left anywhere but the SUV—I locked it back up and turned to get a front view of the townhouse.

I couldn't help but whistle. It didn't sound like Mike had a lot of money so I wondered how he afforded such a nice place. It was a corner home, just past the entrance/exit to the square.

Cypher's information formed a scenario in my head while getting the bags. Mike said Sam smelled the odor of a Changeling on him when they met, meaning he'd been in contact with one. But he claimed the last person he'd seen, other than customers at his store, was Brendi before she disappeared. With this new information, I put together an idea.

I was pretty sure the Fairies, or whatever, had used a Changeling to grab Brendi, and the Changeling killed Teresa and vanished. Given what Cypher said, it should have come after Mike since he was Brendi's dad. So…why hadn't it? Brendi had been gone nearly four months and Mike hadn't mentioned being attacked by a savage animal.

The idea had holes, which I hoped the book in my bag would fill in. When I left Atlanta, a friend gave me a massive tome she called The Big Book of Everything. The thing read like a compendium of the worlds, identifying species, powers, strengths, weaknesses, etc. Seeing the books in the living room reminded me I had it with me. So, maybe this thing would be a bit more informative as to why it hadn't attacked Mike.

And maybe it would give us a clue as to how to get Brendi back.

"Hey Dags?"

I didn't mean to jump, but Sam surprised me. I turned to face her as she came toward me and stood at the back of the SUV. "What's up?"

"Look, I wanted to apologize if I came off as sort of a…well a bitch. I know you want to help, and I think there's a way for you to learn to tap that book. But we just don't have time right now to wait for that to happen. I want you to understand it's nothing personal. Not for me. I think you're a nice kid."

Kid? "I'm nearly the same age as you. Why do you keep calling me a kid?"

She shrugged. "I don't know."

"Well stop it." I turned away and pulled the duffle bag with the book out of my car. I didn't have a good hold of it, so the whole thing hit the pavement and a few things spilled out. I bent over to pick it up and was hit with a serious dizzy spell. Grabbing the back of the SUV I blinked rapidly. The easy diagnosis would be to associate this feeling with the crack to my head. But this felt…different. Something was wrong. Something was…

Here.

"Dags, let me get it. Why don't you go back inside and rest?" Sam knelt down and started picking stuff up.

I turned to try and find what was brushing the edge of my mind. The nagging, dizzy feeling of danger. The street was shaded beneath one of the massive oaks. Spanish moss waved in the cool breeze that chilled the back of my neck. I'd always been good with sensing things around me, even as a kid. So I realized the chill wasn't temperature but the presence of someone close by.

A girl, sixteen or seventeen years old, in a green raincoat, stood on the other side of the hedge bordering the square. She looked familiar and felt all kinds of wrong. Wrong *other* than the fact she was wearing a raincoat and it wasn't raining.

Her blondish hair was cut straight along her brow and hung to her shoulders. The breeze ruffled my hair over my eyes, but hers didn't move. There wasn't any traffic in the square.

In fact, it was eerily quiet.

"Sam—"

"Go on inside before you faint—"

"Hello, Uncle Dags."

That cold feeling I'd had along my neck moved down my spine as I froze beside the SUV. I took a step to the side to instinctively stand in front of Sam. "Sam—" I started again.

"I see it," Sam straightened and moved up beside me. "Go inside."

"Is that the Changeling? It looks sort of like Brendi." If she were wearing Hollywood monster makeup.

"I'm pretty sure."

"Shut up, Witch bitch," the Brendi Monster said in a hiss. "I want *him*." She raised one hand and pointed at me. "And the book."

Book? Did she mean the one on the ground, or the one in my soul? "I know you're not Brendi," I heard myself say. I was trying to think of a way to get away from it.

"I know you know that," she smiled. I didn't like the way it looked. There is nothing spookier than an ill fitted smile, especially one filled with sharp teeth. Her mouth looked like a shark's. "But that's why I wanted to see you. Can't you come into the square and play?" She raised her other hand. In it was a gun. "Come with me, or I shoot the Witch."

In the corner of my vision I saw Sam throw out her hands. They ignited with white blue flame, barely visible in the diffused light through the magnolias. "You can try. Dags, go get Mike."

"No!" Brendi fired.

I thought for sure the bullet would hit Sam, but it didn't. It was met in mid air by something yellowish. If I looked close enough, I thought I saw a tiny naked man. But it was gone as soon as it appeared. And that gunshot was going bring faces to windows in curiosity, which would put everyone in danger.

So I stepped between the two of them. "Wait. Don't shoot again. If you want to talk, we can talk here."

"Dags," Sam hissed. "Get out of my way."

I half turned to answer her. That was a mistake.

The Changeling ran forward and barreled into me. The force knocked me back, but the creature used me as a shield against any attack or defense from Sam. I collided with her, sending us both onto the cobblestone. I turned in time to see the Changeling fire the gun at Sam. Blood splashed against my face and I yelled out as I scrambled to her.

I wasn't fast enough and felt myself fall into darkness when something very hard hit the back of my head.

i SUCK AT MAGiC

When the lights came back on I wasn't in Madison Square anymore. I wasn't even near the SUV or Mike's townhouse.

Hell, I wasn't in Kansas anymore.

The light was dim, like on a cloudy day. Monochromatic. As my eyes adjusted, I could make out what I thought at first was a tunnel in front of me with rounded, carved sides. But when I tried to reach out to touch the sides, I couldn't move.

A much more thorough (and panicked!) examination of my present situation revealed I was tied to a chair. My hands were bound painfully tight behind my back and to the back of the seat. When I moved my fingers around, the ones that weren't already numb, I could feel the chair was wood. It could have been any make of any kitchen chair. Ropes bound my chest to the back as well, wrapped my thighs to the seat, and my ankles were tied to the chair's legs, spread to either side.

Struggling didn't help at all as the muscles in my shoulders and elbows burned with the stress. I looked at the floor. Concrete? Asphalt? It was hard to tell in the dim light—I wasn't even sure where the light was coming from. If I looked to my right another tunnel stretched out into darkness, and there was a duplicate one to my left. I assumed if I could turn around I'd see the same thing behind me. I was in a crossroads, though I wasn't sure what the significance for that was. The chair felt like it was bolted to the spot.

And there was a smell…

"Comfortable, Uncle Dags?"

I froze as the voice echoed around the tunnels. I couldn't figure out where it came from. I couldn't see her and I didn't hear her feet. A part of me was thinking of Sam and hoping she was all right. "Actually, I'm not." I heard the quiver in my voice and hoped like hell she didn't. "Care to tell me why you decided to play kidnap the uncle?"

"Because I knew you wouldn't listen to me any other way," the voice shifted as she spoke, deepening until it matured into a woman's voice. "You see there are some rules we need to establish. I don't like Witches interfering where they're not wanted. I've already suffered losses because of one of your kind. I do not intend on suffering again. I shot the weaker one, but you…there's something familiar smelling about you."

I sensed someone behind me. I could manage a small part of a turn, but it wasn't worth it. A hand gripped my shoulder and applied pressure. I yelled as its fingers dug deeper into my muscle and I could imagine the tips of those fingers as talons tearing through to the bone beneath. Something trickled down my back under my shirt and down my arm, coating my hands and the ropes binding them. I knew it was blood. My blood.

As fast as the hand appeared, it disappeared and I pitched forward against the ropes at my chest. I was sweating—a reaction to the pain and panic. I didn't want to look at my shoulder. I just knew it'd been shredded the way Teresa had been.

My heavy breathing masked her movements until she stood in front of me. She still looked like Brendi in the raincoat, but it definitely wasn't her. "You feel pain. That's good. I enjoy the pounding of your heart, the quickening of your breath. Maybe I shouldn't send a message to that harridan. Maybe I should keep you for myself."

Keep me? I thought about what Cypher had said, about dust and feeding off of humans. I pulled and yanked against the ropes but they weren't giving.

"A little dust and you'll be mine. I could tell you to do anything and you'd do it, little Witch. You'd be my slave for eternity, and die if I abandoned you." She moved in close, nose to nose and that smell. It was like rotting garbage and it permeated everything. "I could control whatever power you have, Witch."

The irony of the situation wasn't lost on me. Here I was, carrying some all-powerful fucked up book in my soul, and no damned way of knowing how to make it work! I watched her stick her hand into her pocket and knew she was going to pull out dust and blow it on me or toss it on me…or something equally terrible.

Okay, think. Calm down and think. All my reading told me spells worked exclusively on intent. It didn't matter what I said or what the ritual was, so long as I knew what I wanted and focused on that. I could shout out the Gettysburg Address and it wouldn't matter as long as I was laser focused on what I wanted.

I closed my eyes and focused everything I could on the idea of getting free. It seemed simple and doable, right? Getting free. I imagined the ropes disappearing. Ropes were made of twine so they could be cut…no don't imagine a knife. With my luck, I'd cut my wrist in the process.

No…I needed to think of something else. Some other way to…

An image of a small book came to me. The book opened and the pages flipped to the right, then the left, as if some unseen hand searched for something specific. Finally, the pages stilled and the book propped itself up for me to see. On that page was the image of what I needed.

And underneath it was a single word, hand written in Sumerian.

Isatum.

Fire.

When I opened my eyes, the Brendi monster was taking her hand out of her pocket. But it didn't matter. Everything slowed down; her movements, my breathing, even the air around me ground to a halt as I opened my mouth and said the word with emphasis, "*Isatum!*"

Instantly, the ropes binding me incinerated—as did my hands, the shirt and the chair, and the ground. The chair's collapse freed me and I screamed at the pain as the rope continued to burn. I fought to get it off of me before I set myself on fire. Scrambling backward and curling my hands against my chest, I turned as I heard someone else screaming.

The Changeling looked like a running torch. Her entire body was engulfed in flames and as she ran around, igniting the walls, the ceiling, everything around her. The fire's heat and strength, conjured by a single word, grew at an alarming rate. I looked at each of the tunnels and picked the one with the brightest light and took off running.

I felt the heat at my back but I was too terrified to turn and look. I imagined it as a thing, chasing me through the tunnels, some creature I'd created, looking for its master. I was breathing heavy, coughing as smoke entered my lungs and my heart thundered against my chest.

Abruptly, I smacked into an iron grate covering a circular exit. Looking past it, I could see the Savannah River and I knew I was still in Savannah…somehow? I had to be in a sewer tunnel or maybe one of the old smuggling passages I'd read about.

I cried out for someone and pushed on the grate—and fell on my face to the cobblestone. Pain radiated out from my hands, my back and my shoulder. It was like someone turned on a pain machine. I looked back at the wall to see if smoke was coming out of the grate—

But the wall was smooth brick. No hole. No grate. No smoke.

But I was apparently smoking. A few tourists ran to me and one lady said, "He's on fire!"

Shivering and unable to form any kind of coherent word, I closed my eyes as I pulled my knees into my chest.

"All right, everyone move out of the way. I need to—holy shit! Who set this kid on fire?"

The voice was male, and very authoritative. I managed to open my eyes and see a Savannah Police Department uniform but little else. My vision was fuzzy around the edges. All I could think about, all I wanted was for the pain to stop.

"Kid," the police officer was close by. "I'm calling an ambulance, okay? Can you tell me who did this to you?"

How was I going to tell a cop that I set myself and a Changeling on fire? With magic? If I weren't in so much pain, I might have come up with some great lie that would work, but I still couldn't manage to talk without shaking.

I heard the sound of a horse's hooves on the infamous River Street cobblestone before I saw it clop in front of the grate. Then I heard a "Whoa," and the sound of boots.

"Hey Thomas. Look, you can't park that here. Gonna need an ambulance so he'll need space to get down here."

"Hello, Officer Declan. It's nice to see you this afternoon. My, my, my…I see. The poor young man is need of medical assistance."

"Yeah, so if you could pull that back up top, I'll move the crowd back—"

"There's no need, Officer. I can handle things here. I can render aid. Why don't you and all these nice folks just go on your merry way and know that this boy will be well taken care of?"

I'd been listening, with my eyes closed, half paying attention. So when this new voice suggested the officer leave and the new voice would take care of me, I opened my eyes again.

A man in a white suit knelt down next to me. I could see the officer walking away, along with what had been a growing crowd of onlookers, come to see the burning man. I narrowed my eyes at the white top hat perched a little sideways on his head. The only splash of color in the whole outfit was a red scarf wrapped around the hat. "You, Mr. McConnell, are in serious need of a healer. Or perhaps, a private place to heal yourself? Your friends have been looking for you."

He looked normal. Dark skin, white goatee, top hat, white tuxedo. I figured he was one of the many horse and buggy services I'd seen all over the Historic District.

I opened my mouth to speak but he shook his head. "No. I'm going to need you to stand. It's going to hurt. I'm afraid most of your shirt is burned away, and most of your skin on your hands and your back…" he shook his head. "Elemental fire is a hard magic to wield."

He helped me up and I hissed and groaned out loud as I leaned heavily on him. I saw the horse and buggy. They were as white and well groomed as he was. "Where did you come from?"

I licked my lips. They were cracked. "…Ho-hole…"

"A hole? Was it in the wall?"

I nodded as we took careful steps to the buggy.

"You came from the Cairn."

Cairn? Was he serious? Cypher had mentioned Cairns. They were the halfway points between this world and a Faerie's world.

My knees gave out from under me and I would have gone down on my knees. The man in the top hat grabbed at my shoulders and I winced when he pressed against the damaged one. I saw stars and he apologized. "Damn boy…I need you to look at me. Can you do that?"

I nodded as I pushed past the wall of pain and folded my arms over my chest, tucking my wrists and hands under my arms.

"Good. Now, did you eat anything?"

Eat? I shook my head.

"Did you get any black dust on you?"

Head shake.

He put two fingers to my neck. "Yeah, you got a pulse. Meaning you got free. But mind you, Medbh's not going to like it you weren't taken. She don't take too kindly to those who get out. Must have done pissed her off for her to take you down that way."

I cleared my throat. It burned. "Medbh?"

"The Winter Queen. Or as she likes it, the Obsidian Queen. The only way you got in that Cairn is because one of her Fae took you in. No one stumbles into that one. She won't allow it."

The Changeling hadn't mentioned the name Medbh. And why would a Faerie queen want me? I figured the Changeling did it on her own.

"Time to get you home."

I nodded. "M-madison Square." I gave him Mike's house number. I remembered it from looking back at the house right before I saw Monster Brendi.

"The shake's coming from the difference in places. Cairn and here don't really go together." He helped me to my feet. My ankles, thighs, chest, wrists, shoulder, everything felt as if it were on fire. I'd managed to burn myself and I didn't really want to see how badly.

Damn, I suck at magic.

I tumbled into his carriage. He waved away a couple as they approached and said in a gentle voice, "Gotta take this boy home. He been down on the street a while. But you kind folk have a nice night, and look up old Thomas Rhymer when you come back by."

i WAS GONE FOR HOW LONG?

I didn't remember anything from the moment Thomas started the carriage to when we arrived at Mike's. What I did remember was thinking the bus driver must've called ahead 'cause Mike was out the door the minute the carriage stopped. I could see him from my prone position in the back but I couldn't really answer him.

Sam helped him get me out and then I was up in his arms in seconds. Did I mention Mike's a big guy?

And I'm not?

Time sort of did this little hide and seek trick after that, from nightmares of seeing those sharp teeth to some dark presence that surrounded me in the street. I wasn't sure if I was reliving what happened when I first saw the Changeling Brendi or if my imagination was on overdrive.

Then everything snapped into place and I sat up, once again naked, once again in the same bedroom.

My wrists, hands and chest were bandaged and my shoulder—

Was smooth. I had to contort my neck into an uncomfortable position but I couldn't see any bandages. I got out of bed and stopped. No dizziness. No need to rush to the bathroom. In fact, I felt better than I had in weeks. I walked to the dresser and examined my shoulder in the mirror. It was whole. Not a mark.

So…had her shredding it been my imagination?

No, it was messed up pretty bad. But Sam fixed it. She concentrated on it instead of the smaller stuff. That's why everything else is healing slowly.

That voice had been in my head. And it was a girl's voice. But it wasn't one I'd heard in that tunnel. In the mirror I saw the wolf step into the doorway and sit, looking up at me.

I narrowed my eyes at its reflection. No…couldn't be.

Could it?

Yeah, it's me. You can hear me now. You've been in a Cairn. In fact, you've been in her *Cairn.*

I turned to face the talking wolf. "Who?"

Medbh. You're lucky you got out. Sam and Mike are downstairs. You guys really need to talk. With that, the wolf got up and loped off.

I braced myself against the dresser and took a deep breath. Sam was downstairs. She was okay.

I just heard a wolf talk to me.

Yep, the Easter Bunny is real.

* * *

I smelled heaven the moment I stepped into the hall after getting dressed and all thoughts of a talking wolf disappeared.

Food.

My stomach roared. The craving nearly bent me over. My bags were in the closet; everything from my hotel room in Garden City was there. The gym bag that'd carried the Big Book of Everything was there, but the book wasn't inside. I hoped to hell the Brendi Monster hadn't taken it when she took me.

I dressed in old jeans and a t-shirt and took the steps two at a time down, my nose leading me all the way.

The table was set with meatloaf, mashed potatoes, green beans, carrots and rolls. Sam was tossing a salad in a large wooden bowl on the far side of the table while Mike sat at the opposite end with my book in front of him. "Oh good…she didn't get the book."

Mike got up and took me into his arms. He squeezed me. Tight. "You have no idea how good it is to see you." Then he put a hand on my arm. "Alive."

"Oh?" I walked toward one of the table settings and looked at him and then Sam. "Are you okay? I thought for sure it killed you."

Sam came out of the kitchen and gave me a hug as well. She looked great. "I'm good. She was a pretty bad shot, even that close. Go ahead and sit down."

I watched her go back to the kitchen before I looked at Mike as he sat back down. "I slept a long time again?"

Sam set the salad forks down and glanced at Mike. He nodded to her. "You've been in bed for two days. But that's actually pretty good for someone who's been in a Cairn. Some people slip into comas and never come out of them."

"Really?" The reality of the situation smacked me in the face. I ran a finger through my hair and realized I hadn't put a comb through it. "I guess if I'd have stayed longer, it would be worse? I was gone for what, a few hours maybe?" I ping-ponged between the two of them. "Why the creepy faces?"

"You were gone for two weeks."

Hear that sound? That was my jaw coming unhinged as it hit the ground. I gripped the back of the chair in front of me and had a flash of being tied to one like it. Every moment of what I believed was little more than a few hours had spanned...*two weeks*?

"Dags sit down before you fall down. Thomas said you didn't eat anything while you were in the Cairn, which means you need to eat now," Sam grabbed a plate and started filling it up. "I'm not kidding. Sit or I'll sit you myself."

I nodded absently as I pulled the chair out and sat. She fixed my plate the way my grandmother used to fix it with a large helping of everything on it. Before I could stop myself, I grabbed a fork and dove into the food. The meatloaf was perfect, the way it melted in my mouth. The green beans still had a bit of snap to them, and the carrots weren't mushy but firm and lightly coated with cinnamon and butter.

Sam poured me a tall glass of sweet tea and placed it in front of me.

Mike continued staring at me. "Slow down."

"He can't. His body needs everything it can find to flush out that nothingness."

They let me eat in peace until the amount of food I'd been shoving in overwhelmed the true size of my stomach. Sam fixed Mike a plate and then one for herself. After several minutes of clinking silverware and my snarfing food, I sat back and grabbed my stomach. "There's no way I was gone for two weeks."

Sam put her fork down and pulled her shirt off of her left shoulder, exposing a longish, nearly healed scar. "That's where she grazed me with the gun."

But—

"For us it was two weeks. But you thought it was a few hours?"

I nodded.

Mike poured himself a glass of tea. "What happened?"

I finished off my tea before I regaled them with finding myself tied to a chair. When I got to the part about the old man in the top hat I stopped. "I…think you know the rest?"

"It fits with what Thomas told us," Mike said. "He said that book called to him. You know you were damn lucky he was near the Cairn exit."

"Yeah." I sat back, even though there was still a half plate of food in front of me. "He asked me about eating while I was in that tunnel, and then if I'd been hit with black dust. It's like he knew what *could* have happened."

"That's because he's been there," Sam said. "Not just in the Cairn, but beyond it. He was once the unwitting guest of the Queen of the Faeries, and when he came out of that place, seven years had passed."

I knew that story. Mom had read it to me several times when I was a kid. "You mean he's *the* Thomas the Rhymer?"

"Yep," Sam picked up her glass of tea. "But now he's a prophet, because that was the gift he chose to take from Tzariene."

"He mentioned Medbh, not Tzariene," I put my hands on the

table. "Why does everyone keep using these names? Medbh? Tzariene? It's like the land Shakespeare created."

"He didn't create the names," Mike shrugged. "He just used them. The Courts of the Faerie are pretty much the way we've read them. Only they're called Silver and Obsidian. Tzairene is Silver and Medbh's Obsidian. But she's also known as Maab."

I ran my tongue over my teeth. I needed my toothbrush. "Before I went to the car, I was researching Changelings. Spoke to a guy I've known a few years. He's the one that said Faeries weren't happy little creatures with wings."

"They're not," Mike wiped his mouth with his napkin. "He tell you about real Changelings?"

I relayed what Cypher had said and what I'd observed about the Brendi Monster. "I'm gonna go out on a limb here and guess you both already knew this?"

"Parts of it," Sam pursed her lips. "Neither of us had seen the Changeling to know for sure that's what attacked Teresa, but given my own experience with Medbh, it all fit the profile."

"You've dealt with her?" I blinked at Sam. I'd noticed earlier her face seemed brighter and realized she wasn't wearing any makeup. Her hair was up in a ponytail that hung past her shoulders.

"As a Witch, I'm not partial to the Faerie Kingdoms."

"The Changeling called *me* a Witch, but I figured she assumed that's what I was because you helped me."

"No—it didn't assume you were a Witch. You *are* a Witch. It's in your blood. Probably carried from your mother."

I swallowed. "I don't know much about my mom."

"Really? You and I have something in common then," Sam sipped her tea. "My mom was a Witch, same as me. But she died when I was eight. I was trained by my aunt."

"I wasn't trained by anyone."

Mike spoke up. "Dags's past is somewhat of a mystery."

"You mean the tree?"

I shrugged. "More than that. I can't remember anything before waking up in a long-term care facility. I'd been in a coma for nearly a year after the house burned down. They said Mom was killed in the fire. I disappeared and a neighbor said they saw me running into the woods. But it took them a while to find me because I was inside of a tree."

"When you say inside—"

"*Inside*. The tree had grown around me. Not placed around me. Grown. A helicopter running an infrared spotted my heat signature. Confused the hell out of the searchers, not only because they couldn't readily see me but also the pilot swore his team had gone over that area for five days before I showed up. They had to chop up the tree, carefully saw me out. I was asleep, woke up screaming and then," I shrugged. "Coma."

"And you can't remember anything."

"Nothing. I can't even remember my mom's face," I leaned forward and put my elbows on the table. "I remember a locket around her neck. It had a red stone on it and a wolf and moon. I thought it was beautiful. They never found it."

"And your dad?"

"My parents had divorced six months earlier. The police tried to pin the fire on him. Called it domestic violence. I never believed it. But he didn't have time for some sick kid so he put me in a facility. When I woke up he put me with nannies, and when I was ten in boarding school. I think I've seen him maybe…a dozen times since then."

"That's freak'n sad," Sam said. "So you've had the God Mother's blood and never knew it."

"I knew something was weird. I could see ghosts and weird shit. But I learned real fast not to tell people."

Mike laughed. "I bet. He didn't tell me right away."

"No. So I guess I should start learning to be a Witch?" It was a loaded question. No one had asked me how I got burned yet, and I didn't want to tell them I'd tried using that magic and ended up barbecuing myself.

"You were *supposed* to be a Witch. But your course went off track somewhere," she sat forward. "I'm guessing the moment you allowed the Cruorem to brand you with those portals is when it happened." She nodded to my hands. "And I'll bet you Bonville didn't come after you because you were a tool in his little cog-work of magical mayhem. I bet he went after you because he knew what you were and he wanted to harness your power."

I rubbed at my face and glanced at Mike. "You got all this?"

"Sort of. I just want Brendi back. And after the shit I've seen, I'm willing to believe anything that proves to me she's not dead."

"Brendi is also a Witch," Sam said and I looked back at her. "And I'm more sure than ever that's why Medbh fashioned a Changeling to take her."

"What for?"

"Faeries love to take Witches. Make us into Hunt Beasts. As a Beast we can't use our magic. We can't fight them and stop them from entering this world. We can manifest events, items and we can bend them. Some of us, like myself, can actually commune with the Elementals and work within their power for magic. For a Faerie to create a Cairn takes over a hundred human souls. For an Ethereal, or Angel, to create a Power, they kill a human. For an Abysmal creature, or Demon, to obtain physical form, they have to kill their host, and don't tell me the Revenants aren't dead. Once those creatures are attached to those humans the humans can't survive without them. They're as good as dead. Do you see the pattern?"

She leaned forward and put her elbows on the table. "If one of these Angels or Demons can take control of a Witch, they would have the ability to create multiple openings between the worlds with no restrictions. The very things we can close, we can open."

"But aren't Cairns fixed?" I leaned forward as well, even though my stomach protested. I was really full. "The one I just came out of is always there, right? I got the impression from Thomas that's Medbh's Cairn?"

"Yes. The Faeries can make a *fixed* Cairn, but the problem for them is the Cairns themselves. As they are now, without the magic of a Witch, they trap the Faerie. The Cairn is the closest they can come to our world, because of the safety protocols in place. But the Cairns are just as much of a trap to them as they are to us. What happened to you physically is just a shadow of what would happen to them if they entered those Cairns, and then returned home."

"The shakes, the fever, the sickness?"

"Much worse for them. Some of them die if they return to where they come from. And as for stepping through that gate to this world?" Sam snapped her fingers. "Ash."

"But no ash if they make it using a Witch."

"Right."

"But, it's been what, months since Brendi vanished?" I looked at Mike. "Why hasn't she used your daughter to make one of these gates? Or has she?"

Sam answered. "She hasn't. We're not sure why that is. Might be the Changeling has to kill off everyone that knew her. Could be Brendi doesn't want to do it. I just don't have those answers." Now Sam fixed me with a hard stare. "How did the fire start? You didn't see Medbh and the Changeling didn't mention her. But I don't think Changelings have that kind of power."

I stared at my hands. Do I tell the two of them I was the one that started the fire? The fact I was able to access the book was a good thing, and it might boost their confidence in me. But then telling them I'd set everything on fire might null and void everything. I knew they were still trying to find Brendi, and I was more determined than ever to help them, whether they wanted me or not.

"I don't know," I shrugged. "I was in so much pain I didn't see it coming."

Neither of them asked any more questions and I didn't volunteer any more answers.

THE BiG BOOK OF EVERYTHiNG

Apparently, after the Changeling wounded Sam and took me, Mike and Sam spent days searching. They knew for sure it was a Changeling now and focused their search on where it would have taken me. Sam worried I'd been taken to the Faerie Realm. No one really knew where that realm was or how to get there because Cairns were so well disguised.

Mike and Sam had met Thomas Rhymer their first night searching for signs of Brendi on the streets of Savannah and agreed with Sam's belief the girl had been taken by Faerie. Thomas had told them there were a few Cairns in the area but he couldn't open them. That happened only when the time was right. He did say their realm was known as *Alfheim* and if one of the Queens, possibly Medbh, had instructed the Changeling to take me, then he was pretty sure I would end up a Hunt Beast.

Mike said, "I had this nasty idea that if Brendi refused to help them, they'd take you and then threaten her life to force you to build the Cairn for them."

We were cleaning up the dishes, still talking. It was just after seven in the evening and the garden in the back rested in shadows. Sam washed, I dried and Mike put things away, dishes and leftovers. The whole scene felt so surreal, given what just happened. I lowered the plate and towel in my hand. "Why didn't they?"

Sam paused and looked at me. "Why didn't they what?"

"Force me to build a Cairn like you said? The Changeling sensed the same thing about me that she apparently sensed in Brendi. She called me Uncle Dags, so I assume she knew that much about mine and Brendi's relationship. So, why not take me further in than the Cairn? Why not try and use me if I'm a Witch?"

Sam's expression was hard to read as she stared at me. "That's a very good question. But I don't have an answer. She took you to a crossroads and tied you to a chair."

"Yeah."

When she grabbed a towel and dried her hands, I set the plate I was drying on the counter as Mike stood to her right.

"What is it?" Mike asked.

"It's just that...the symbol of the crossroad has an almost universal meaning. In most religions and faith-based practices around the world, a crossroad represents a place where several worlds connect. Not so much like a Cairn door or gate, but more of a junction. Four paths converging at a single point."

I looked past her to Mike, who shrugged.

Sam caught the gesture and held out her hands. "It's symbolic meaning is that someone is standing on the threshold. They've come to the middle, a place where a decision must be made. It's not as eloquent as say crossing the Rubicon, but the meaning's the same."

I wasn't sure I knew what the Rubicon was. "I get the symbology—but why put me there?" I leaned against the counter. "You think the Changeling did it on her own? Or was it something Medbh told her to do?"

"Changelings carry the essence of both their creator and the subject they're created from. Maybe..." Sam shrugged. "Maybe she sensed you're undecided. That you've not actually chosen one path over the other. Some call you a Guardian, I called you a Witch...the Grimoire inside of you might be causing interference. On a base level, the Changeling didn't know what you were so she placed you in the crossroads."

I arched an eyebrow at her. "For?"

She gave a long sigh. "I don't know. I'm not sure the actions of a Changeling are relevant to finding Brendi. What we have to know more about is the Cairn you were in," Sam looked at me. "Are you familiar with Cairns?"

"I know a little about them because of my mother."

"She liked Faeries?"

I snorted and handed Mike a plate. "She was more like terrified of them. She always had me spell the word differently. F. A. E. R. I. E. said the other way, the F. A. I. R. Y. was just the laymen's understanding of them. I remember gardeners coming to the house every day to make sure there weren't any Cairns that popped up overnight. I think at first they all humored her, but then after a while I noticed a few of them stopped coming and the others were a bit less jovial."

"What does that mean?" Mike set a plate in the cabinet.

"Oh, like I said, at first they used to kid with me about my mom. Crazy woman. Scared of little Faeries. That kind of thing. But they stopped doing that and started whispering to themselves before they stopped coming period."

Sam turned back to the sink. "What kind of garden did your mom have?"

"An English garden—a lot like the one Mike's got out back." I stared out the window. I tried to call up those old images of mine, the ones of me playing ball around the fountain. I always liked the fountain because it had koi in it. I said as much to Sam and Mike. "I never saw mom buy the fish, and I never saw the gardeners bring them either. They just multiplied."

"They call that sex, Dags."

I gave Mike a foul look. "That's not what I mean. Something my mom said stuck with me when I asked about them having babies. She said all the fish were male. We could tell that because the males were the prettiest."

Sam looked at the murky water in the sink. "You ever noticed a correlation between the increase in fish and decrease in gardeners?"

"No." And then I jumped on her train of thought. I snapped my head around and stared at her. "You think the gardeners turned into fish?"

"Depends on what Faerie claimed that garden."

"I thought you said they couldn't come into this world or they turn to ash?"

She pushed her hand into the water and retrieved the wash towel. "They can't. But they can send out little minions. Creatures loyal to them. Sort of like…"

"Fetches?" I asked.

Sam gave me a smirk as she looked at me. "Yeah. Only in my opinion, they're more insidious. The usual Fetches, the ones made by magic, seem a little brain dead. You know, they got one mission and that's all they got? Well, try coming up on a slug, or a purblind, and not to mention…." she made a face. "A redcap."

I looked over at Mike. He shook his head. "Don't look at me. I have no idea what she's talking about."

"You both need to read that book Dags brought. It's one hell of a book of knowledge. In fact, I need to look up crossroads. But," she said and pointed to the clock over the stove before she dried her now wet hand again. "We've got very little time if we're going to make work of the full moon."

Again, Mike and I glanced at each other before we followed Sam out of the kitchen. She stopped at the dining room table where the BBOE (that's the Big Book of Everything) lay open. She moved a few of the pages. "I found a spell to trap and hold a Fae."

Again, Mike and I shared glances. "Sam," I said. "Fae? Fairy? Same thing?"

"No. A Faerie is what Medbh is. They're the indigenous whatsis of their race. But their creations, the ones I was just telling you about, the ones that can manifest and move about in this world, are what we call Fae. They're like aberrations of their creators," she paused. "Like the Changeling."

"Ah," Mike nodded. "I get it."

I didn't but...meh.

"Dags, all those names I just said? Those are Fae. Compare them to the Revenants or Powers. They possess the same cognitive power of thought as a living creature."

How did she know I wasn't following? Was it written on my face? Or was she just assuming I was too simple to get it? "And you know the difference because they're here in this world."

"Hon." She put a hand on my shoulder. The touch was electrical. I felt it all over my body. If it affected her the same way, she didn't show it. "Fae creatures aren't like anything you've ever seen in this world. Changelings are the closest to something...*normal* looking."

I thought of the Changeling's teeth. That was *not* normal looking.

Mike sat down near the book. "Are you wanting to trap one?"

"I'd like to trap that Changeling if it comes back. Question it."

I got a flash of it running around and burning. "And you want to see if it knows where Brendi is?"

"They wouldn't tell us even if they knew." She turned the book to face Mike and myself. "In order to get Brendi from Medbh, we're going to need two things. Proof. We can't just charge at this blindly. We have a great hypothesis, but we need to locate Brendi. Second, if she is with Medbh, then we'll need something to trade. I'm not sure it'll work, but I thought if we had something Medbh really wanted..." she looked at each of us. "She might do a swap. I looked into this wonderful book of yours and found some information about a mantle, a simple piece of cloth, given to Medbh by Oberon when they were lovers. Legend says it was made of the stars and woven by spiders—which sort of creeps me out."

Me too.

"The mantle was stolen not long after Oberon replaced Medbh with Tzariene. Medbh vowed a wish to whomever found her mantle."

"No one's found it?" Mike leaned back in the chair.

"Nope. It's slipped into legend. I've never heard about it. And I'm sure no one else has either."

"So...." he raised his arms and tucked his hands behind his head. "How exactly do we find a mantle spun by spiders?"

I nearly choked when she turned and pointed at me. "Him."

"Me? I don't know where to find a mantle. I've never heard of it either."

"Right. But," she said and bent over the book and flipped few pages. I leaned over with her and caught the section header: *Finder*. Oh boy. "See here? It says there are spells to find things, but no one ever listed any of them in this book."

"Maybe that's because it's not always wise to go looking for some... things?"

"Maybe. But I'm pretty sure the Grimoire has one of those basic magic spells the Big Book of Everything mentions," she smiled at me and I backed up again when she wiggled her eyebrows. "Time to put yourself to good use, other than sapping all my healing power."

"It's not like I asked to get beaten up."

"Man-up bro," her eyes sparkled.

"Wait just a minute," Mike leaned forward and lowered his arms. "You think maybe the Changeling sensed the book? It knew what it was?"

Sam nodded. "I think it was confused, which would explain the use of the crossroads and not taking him straight to Medbh. That's my theory. He has the smell and feel of one of the God Mother's children. But he's been tainted with other magic, like the Cruorem brandings as well as the Grimoire. But he's also like a child holding a loaded weapon. He's not been trained with what he has. He's low hanging fruit."

Now that was just mean.

"So we need to find a way to communicate with that book, right now. We need a spell to find this mantle. So, you're on, sunshine."

Mike chuckled. "I think you freaked him out."

Sam moved closer to me and put a warm hand on my cheek. "Darren McConnell, you were chosen by fate to carry this book. You keep it from the hands of everyone else by holding it to your soul. It's why they call you a Guardian now, because you keep the book's secrets safe."

"I don't think the Witch that put it there did it for those reasons."

"Doesn't matter. It's done. So you accept it and you make the best of it," she stepped back. "So now I have to ask you…is there a way for you to look into the book?"

Did I tell her I had? That I found a spell for fire and nearly burned myself alive? "Uh…not that I know of."

"Then let's try. No harm in that, right?"

No. Unless you want to blow up Mike's townhouse.

She pursed her lips. "Maybe if you try it now and think of a spell to find…." she paused as if looking for the right word. "Well, I can't say find Fae objects or we'll be scrounging through a bazillion items. Those little fuckers are hoarders by nature. So…how do we narrow it down?"

I gave it a bit of thought. I could understand saying Dark objects or Light. But since we didn't know where they were from, it sort of limited us. "How about I look for lost objects from a lover?"

Mike snorted. "That sounds like asking to empty a junk closet. You'll end up getting everything but the kitchen sink."

"You got a better idea?" she gave him a withering look and then looked back at me. "Try it. What do we have to lose?"

I really don't like those words. It's like saying…"Hey Murphy! Fuck with me!"

I closed my eyes and tried to think with the same intensity I did in the Cairn. I figured if I could do it again, with the two of them with me, and this was successful then they wouldn't be so worried about me helping them. I didn't want to escape this time, I needed to *find* something. I thought of the feeling I had when I lost my mom's locket. I understood the desire to find something.

I'd wanted it for over fifteen years.

I heard Sam gasp in the distance but ignored it. The book appeared to me again, closed just like before. But this time it flipped open to a page filled with words. All kinds of words. So I started reading them aloud. And as I read them I committed them to memory. I knew I would never forget this spell, just like I would never forget the one for fire.

And when the spell was finished, the book closed.

"Wow," I said as I blinked a few times. But Sam and Mike had their jaws hanging open. "What?"

"You…." Sam pointed. "It came out of your chest. It was all glowing and ghostly. You had it in your hands and turned the pages. Then… you stopped, and started reading from it."

"Really?" I remembered reading; I just thought it was in my head. "What'd I say?"

Mike gave a nervous laugh. "Who knows? You were talking in some weird language. Couldn't understand a word."

"Sumerian," I looked around. "You got a pen and paper?"

She brought me her iPad, and for the next twenty minutes I translated the spell in my head into English. When I was done, we all whistled. Some of it was an ingredients list and the rest was a simple ritual.

"I've got most of these things…but," she said and pointed to one of the items on the screen. "What the hell is a 'three day dead shroud of a respected woman?'"

I looked at it again. "Uh…"

"You got that wrong," she arched her eyebrow at me.

"No, I didn't."

"Yeah, you did. That doesn't make any sense."

Mike took the tablet and started poking at it.

"Sam, I didn't get it wrong. The thing is burned into my brain and that's what the translation says."

"Translations can be wrong. I mean, look at the Bible and the whole prostitute thing—"

"I'm not having a debate with you," I stood up and faced her. "The list isn't wrong. Just break it down. You have to find the shroud of a woman who's been dead for three days, and that woman has to have led a respectable life."

She put her hands on her hips. "And where in the hell in the city of Savannah do you think we're going to find that?"

"Right here."

We both turned and looked at Mike as he turned the tablet to face us.

"Mrs. Jessica Reinhold, passed away two days ago from complications of a knee replacement. She was fifty-three and an upstanding lady of Savannah. See? Her obituary says she was a member of the Mayflower Society."

I grabbed the tablet and skimmed the obituary. "Fuck…it says her funeral was today, where she was interned in her family mausoleum in Bonaventure Cemetery."

"Yay. Great. That place gives me the creeps," Sam crossed her arms over her chest.

"You don't get it," I turned the tablet to face her. "She died *two* days ago. This is the third day. Some traditions bury on the third day. She died at eleven twenty two p.m. We've got less than five hours to find her and get her shroud before she's dead *four* days. Otherwise, we're going to have to wait for another upstanding lady to pass away."

Mike stood up. "I hate cemeteries…"

BONAVENTURE

I'm not sure if I mentioned it before, but I'm not fond of cemeteries either. Especially not the kind where all the gravestones are sculptures and big box mausoleums with doors. Too Hollywood. Too...*something's going to come out and eat me* feeling.

Just like the other cemetery I'd been in two weeks ago. I'd looked at a grave and something *did* come out and try to eat me.

An Angel.

It took just over half an hour to get to Bonaventure. But it was closed, which meant the large gates leading into the infamous cemetery were locked. Wasn't it fortuitous that Grey the wolf-dog knew another way in?

A cold feeling of dread ran up my spine once we climbed under the fence. My face stung from the scratches inflicted by the thick hedging blocking the hidey-hole. Sam turned on a penlight and moved it along the ground. We decided early on the use of light had to be limited. People lived around the cemetery and any kind of light would be visible. It was a waxing moon, so what light did filter through the thick canopy of oaks protecting the cemetery was bright enough to see by.

Sort of. If you were a bat. With radar.

"So...which way do we go?" I looked around.

"I don't know," Sam moved the tiny beam of light over my boot. "I thought you two knew where this woman's grave was."

I gave her a pretty hateful look and was happy she couldn't see my face. "They don't have addresses for gravestones in obituaries."

Mike didn't say anything as he followed Grey. He had a backpack on and pulled out one of his Desert Eagles. Sam pulled at my t-shirt and we followed the big guy around the footpaths.

We entered near a huge Celtic cross and moved toward the water. The cemetery backed up along the Savannah River. I'd been here once or twice as a kid, long before any movies were made about good and evil. And the place still gave me the same *heebee jeebees* it did when I was six. I think what really gave the place character—other than the Spanish moss that hung like beards off the trees—was the array of monuments. I'd seen the piano headstone before, and the creepy little crib one. There were several that looked like kids. And a pyramid, which just failed to make any sense to me.

But the creepiest kinds in my opinion, especially out here in that moon-doused, monochromatic light, were the angels. They were everywhere. Wings folded in, heads bowed, and hands usually out in supplication. I don't know why—but they scared me the most.

My nanny thought it was some kind of child psychosis, my dislike of angels. Imagine explaining that to your church going friends—about how the kid you watched screamed when he saw an image of an angel.

Thinking of Gabriel, maybe my younger self knew something I hadn't even realized yet.

When we reached a main road where a car or tour bus could drive, Sam stopped and thumped the back of Mike's shoulder. "Hey," she hissed. "We're going in circles."

"I'm following the wolf," Mike gestured to the animal in the middle of the road. "She's sniffing."

I looked around us, keeping close. It was sort of odd to me, that I could look around the cemetery from any vantage point and see the tombstones and mausoleums on the opposite end. A waist high level of azaleas dotted the empty spaces.

To my right I could just see the river through the trees. The moon sparkled on its surface, giving the whole night a surreal moment to it. But then…I was in a cemetery after eight in the evening…looking for a freshly buried nice old lady. Not sure how much more surreal I could get.

"What if she's in one of these mausoleums?" Sam whispered. "These things have locks."

"They do?" I looked at her. "Why? Who's going to steal anything out of—" and then our present circumstance came crashing on top of my head. "Oh."

That's when I noticed Mike was a few feet down the road with Grey. Sam and I ran to catch up. "Where are you going?"

He stopped and pointed to the left. "She's heading through there. Just past the Mercer grave. I see a hell of a lot of wreaths."

Genius.

We tromped around the footpaths toward the flowers and Sam groaned once we arrived. "Fuck…it *is* a mausoleum."

I heard a low growl and looked down. Grey stood between Sam and I and she was giving the mausoleum in the distance a really nasty evil eye. The thing was still a good fifty feet away, but even in the moonlight I could see why she didn't like it.

The outside of the small marble structure was the centerpiece of a plethora of flowers. Standing wreaths, O's with sashes across the middle and a few solid hearts. The basket and oasis flower arrangements were stacked at least six rows away from the front doors, making it look like a little garden.

When Sam started forward, I grabbed her arm. "Why is Grey not happy?"

"I have no idea. It's okay," she tried to pull away. "If you're afraid, stay here."

I ignored that. A movement amid all those petals made me grip her arm tighter. "She might not be wrong. Hey Mike…come back here."

I led them several feet back the way we came into a plot with a Roman column tombstone. The column gave us a bit of shielding and a great vantage point. Once they knelt down next to me, Sam shot me an irritated look. "What are you afraid of?"

I started to answer but Mike put his finger to his lips and then pointed.

All four of us leaned forward to see under the moonlight. A few of the potted arrangements were moving on the right side. I don't mean their leaves shifted in the breeze. I mean their leaves and vines *moved* like limbs. The three-legged stands bent, transforming into spindly legs, as the smaller potted arrangements grew stems and leaves toward the ground to push themselves along.

I felt Grey move beside me, another low growl deep in her throat.

"Fae," Sam sighed.

"What the hell kind of Fae are *those*?" Mike whispered. "It's like the funeral flowers are alive. And I don't mean that flowers aren't alive, it's just that...." he didn't finish the sentence but gestured.

Didn't matter. I got his meaning.

"I'm pretty sure they're *fir darrig* (she pronounced it fear deang). Or they could be goblins or bogles. Depends on who summoned them."

I glanced from her to the moving plants. "Summoned them for what? I mean...why are there Fae outside of some old woman's mausoleum? Was she connected to them in some way?"

"I don't think so," Sam's expression paled even under the moonlight. "Shit...unless somehow someone or something already knows what we're up to."

"You mean Medbh?"

"Possibly...but for her to know, she'd had to have some means of listening in on our conversation at Mike's. But I warded the whole place against magical interference."

I looked at each of them before settling back on Sam. "So...what do you want to do? Either way we have to get into that tomb."

"We still have a little time," Mike said, a bit more relaxed than I wanted him to be. He had the guns. I had a temperamental magic book and a childhood fear of things moving that weren't supposed to. Like plants. And dolls.

Mike smirked at me. "Dags doesn't like things moving that aren't supposed to."

"What does that mean?" Sam said.

"You know, if dolls or plants move."

Sam looked at me. "Venus flytraps must render you catatonic."

I ignored both of them and then shifted my position so I could get a better look. Grey moved back a little. It looked like the larger standing arrangements, the kind I remembered from childhood with three wire-framed legs, moved into position in front of the door. And the smaller, creepier ones took up positions in front of them. "It looks like a chess board."

"What?"

I pointed. "Look, there's a king and queen in the back, those two flanking over there look like rooks, and in front are the pawns—" I did a mental recount. "Hey…aren't a few of them missing?"

"How can you tell?"

"Because I remember one that had roses and now I don't see—"

Grey barked and growled. *Loud.*

"What the—!" Sam hissed beside me—and then disappeared.

I turned to see her flail backwards as something started dragging her away. Grey launched into the air to follow, snapping at something above Sam's head.

"Holy shit! A rose plant's got her!" Mike jumped up and grabbed her ankles and tried to stop her from slipping under a grove of azaleas.

Seriously? Man killer plants?

I scrambled toward her shoulders in time to see vines wrap around her neck. She tried to scream, maybe even repeat a spell, but the thing was choking off her air. Her attacker was the rose arrangement, and the flower's leaves had grown out to take hold of her. I reached past her shoulder and grabbed at the base of the plant. The thing was rooted in a florist's oasis, that spongy thing they used to hold the flowers in place. But when I put my fingers inside, it felt more like I was squeezing something very wet, very cold and very nasty.

"Dags look out!"

Mike's warning came just in time as one of the vines lashed out at *my* neck. I ducked to the right and squeezed whatever the hell I had a hold of as hard as I could, imagining it pop like a grape. The vine grazed my arm and I felt its thorns take off skin just as Grey lunged and snapped half of it off in her jaw. With a hiss I straddled Sam the best I could by sliding one leg under her shoulders just in front of the plant and the other over her chest to get her in a scissor lock. Then I reached down and grabbed at the vines encircling her throat. They were tight and Sam's eyes were rolling back. Damn thing was going to suffocate her before I could pry it off.

Something stung my face as I pulled, yanked and squeezed. I hadn't noticed the baby's breath decorating the roses. Tiny little white flowers that would normally compliment the red of the rose now sported some serious little choppers and were biting the shit out of any piece of skin they could get hold of.

Between my constant swearing and Grey's barking, we could forget the element of surprise.

"Mike," I said through gritted teeth. The other half of the vine I'd ducked and Grey snagged was back and wrapping itself around my chest. If it got to my neck I was going to have to let go. "I need.... *help*..."

His response was a series of grunts. I chanced a look back at the Roman column headstone. Mike had problems of his own. He'd tossed his backpack off and was dueling one of the three-legged arrangements. It was using one of its legs to jab and parry and Mike was using the biggest and longest damn knife I'd ever seen. Had he pulled *that* out of his bag? How deep did that thing go? The arrangement had lost a lot of flowers, the oasis visible in the mess. But Mike was sporting a good many bloody points over his shoulders and chest and a ripped shirt. The fighting monstrosity was holding its own.

The vine made it to my neck and I had to let go of the one wrapping around Sam's. I grabbed the end of it and stopped it from completing the circle, but the thing in my other hand began to burn my palm. Either my hand was on fire or the plant...

On fire…

I *could* set the plant on fire. But what if I set the entire cemetery on fire as well? What if I set Mike or Sam or even Grey on fire, making them a moving torch? Images of the running, burning Changeling came back to me as the vine trying to make a nice choker around my neck tightened. My legs were still wrapped around Sam's chest, under her arms, but the plant trying to drag her off started dragging both of us.

I didn't know what else to do. I didn't have a weapon and I didn't have any other spell and I sure as hell didn't have time to consult the Grimoire. Maybe…maybe if I concentrated my will carefully while being choked, I could just make it burn the plant…

"Isatum!"

This time I had a clear visual in my head, pure intent, of what I wanted burned. And I wanted it burned down to nothing. The thing stopped its movements in seconds because every part of it glowed a brilliant yellow gold and then blood red. Two seconds more and the entire rose arrangement was little more than black ash, burning from the inside.

And this time I hadn't burned myself! Or even more importantly, Sam.

She gasped and lay on her back, her hands to her neck. I fell back but knew I couldn't stay there. With a groan, I rolled over on my side and touched her arm. "You…okay?" I was out of breath. Wasn't used to all this exercise. That and I'd noticed when I used that spell I felt a little tired.

She nodded but her eyes widened. I turned to look behind me. The three-legged arrangement charged me. I held up my right hand at it. *"Isatum!"*

Poof. It had momentum but by the time it reached Sam and I, there was little left but ash.

"When the hell did you learn to do that?" Mike pulled me onto my feet and then knelt over Sam. "And if you could do that, why didn't you just set the whole garden of them on fire?"

I wanted to answer, but Sam beat me to it as she rubbed her neck. "You saw why. Remember the burns on him when Thomas brought him back?"

I felt her eyes on me and averted my own gaze.

"Jesus Dags, you burned yourself?"

"You were trying to get away? That's how you escaped?" Sam said.

I nodded but stepped back. I held out my hands. "Look—you saw what I did to myself. I think I set fire to the whole place. I wasn't kidding when I said I ran from the fire. And I did it." There wasn't anything I could really say or do and I wanted them to stop looking at me. "It was too powerful."

"We can talk about this later," Sam said. "Just know that the expenditure of power can be triggered by emotional stress. And if she was hurting you, it's understandable. For right now, tell me what it was you said."

Shrugging I said, "I said the Sumerian word for fire. The book showed me when I asked—"

"That's how you knew to look for the finder spell," Mike said. "You son of a bitch. You already knew what you were doing."

"No I didn't. I don't!" I glanced over at the remaining plants. They were heading our way. "You saw what I did to myself. It wasn't just me I set on fire."

Sam turned, also aware of the approaching CGI nightmare of plants. Grey pattered up beside me and I saw her ready herself in a pouncing stance. Good girl. "Dags, you said you used the word fire. Can you try a bit more control and use a word for it?"

"Word for it?"

"Yeah, instead of using the word in a broad sense, corral it. Use another Sumerian word that works for you and do something about the botanical nightmare heading our way."

I faced the approaching horde. If I were by myself, I might actually scream and run like a little boy out of the cemetery. But with the two of them there, this might work. I opened my mouth to speak but Sam stopped me with a touch on my shoulder. "Use your hand. Like you did with the plant that attacked you. Direct the spell."

"Spell?"

"It's a spell, Dags."

I raised my hand and the phrase I needed came to me. *"Isatum sihirtu."* Burn them all.

Every one of them exploded, burned and then drifted into little piles of black dust. I thought I did pretty well. Didn't even singe the ground. Unfortunately, I had a moment of dizzy and might have fallen on my ass if Mike hadn't grabbed me.

"You okay?"

I nodded. "Yeah. Let's get this shroud and get the fuck out of here so I can take a nap." I shrugged him off, aware of Sam behind us. In fact, I'd started noticing her all the time. Not in like a she's a good looking woman way, but in a *presence* way. I could close my eyes and know where she was. Even at Mike's townhouse I knew what room she was in. Was that some weird link because we were Witches? We had the God Mother's blood?

I shrugged it off and strode to the front of the mausoleum. The doors were tall and thin. I estimated that if they were opened, the width would just about accommodate a coffin and little else. They were solid, not stained glass or ornate iron like some of the others in the cemetery. Mike moved ahead of me and produced a penlight from his back pocket. He shined it on the door handle. The right door was ajar.

He opened it.

Something heavy, slippery, cold and smelling of charred flesh flew out of it, violently knocking Mike backward before it leapt on top of me. We both went backward and the thing managed a death grip around my arms and chest. The fall to the ground knocked the wind out of me so I couldn't yell out anything. Too late, I realized what it was.

The Changeling. Only it was little more than a charred corpse.

Within seconds the thing had its long, sharp teeth buried into my neck while it's claws raked along my stomach.

My screams echoed inside of Bonaventure.

AM i ALiVE?

I think in the back of my head, remembering the burning Changeling, I thought I'd killed it. I thought there was no way it could survive that kind of burn. But here it was, killing me. And there wasn't a spell in my head to stop it.

I heard Mike and Sam yelling and Grey's angry barking and snarling. Sam's voice rose above the wolf's as she recited something. I caught a flash of blue white light, felt something cold on top of me and then the Changeling wasn't there anymore. Not that it mattered. The fear of dying had my full attention. The pain was like a fire of its own. I put my hand to my neck, touched something wet, and held it in front of me. In the moonlight I saw my palm covered in something dark and slick.

"Dags…stop. Don't touch it. Don't move," Mike knelt over me and had his hand on my forehead. "Jesus…oh god damn it…Sam look at it."

"Where is it?" Sam's voice was tight as she moved beside me. "I found it." She appeared just before the penlight came on. The beam focused on my chest and then my neck. Breathing was becoming difficult as something filled my throat. I coughed and tasted blood. A lot of it. I felt it trickle over my cheeks as it came from my mouth.

"This is what Teresa looked like," Mike said in a soft voice. "That's the thing that killed her. Oh god…I really didn't want to believe it, that something that looked like Brendi could do this…."

"Mike, you have got to rein it in," her voice cracked a little. I knew she was panicking. I was too. The pain crescendoed to a roaring blaze in my chest as I coughed up more blood and decided it was a better idea to lie still and die.

No Darren…they will not let you die.

The voice was familiar. It was Grey again. I'd forgotten I'd heard her before. I hadn't even mentioned it to Sam or Mike. "You…I can hear you…"

"What?" Mike leaned in close. His face was a little bleary. "You can hear me?"

Yes. You need to release the Grimoire so they can save your life. The book protects you as you protect it.

It does? I wasn't sure how to release it. And it was getting harder to stay focused and concentrate. The pain became a numbing wall around me.

The Changeling's venom will kill you even if the blood loss doesn't. Darren, just open the book for her.

Open the book for who?

The answer came to me through the fog and I felt my chest unclench.

"Sonofa—do you *see* that? It's doing what it did in the townhouse."

"Mike, stand back. Let me get in there."

I refocused and saw light moving over Mike and Sam. Floating in the air a few feet above me was that small, delicate book. The light from it illuminated Sam's face as she knelt before it. The light moved from white to blue to gold and then to white again. Tiny sparkles danced around her face and I coughed. "Say…the words…."

"Say the words? But…I don't know Sumerian!"

It didn't matter. Intent was all that mattered. And she, as a Witch, should know that. I closed my eyes.

Sam's voice rang out across the vast darkness behind my eyelids. And as she repeated the spell in a language long dead, images of people came to me. They came so fast I couldn't name them, and when the spell was done, I heard a woman crying.

"Dags?"

A hand moved my shoulder back and forth. I reached up and batted at them. "No…uh uh…ten more minutes."

Someone snorted. "He's fine."

Mike? I opened one eye, then the other. "What time is it?"

He arched a dark brow at me. "Can you sit up?"

I pushed myself up on my elbows and then he helped me into a sitting position. Sam sat a few feet away, her hands against her face. I saw little orbs of primary colors moving around her. Red, blue, green and yellow. "Sam?"

"Give her a minute. She said she wasn't used to using that kind of power."

Barking and snarling to my right caught my attention. Grey had the little Changeling monster corralled against a tree. A pentagram glowed around the base of the tree and the Changeling. I looked down at my shirt. It was bloody and torn to shreds, but the skin beneath it was smooth and white. I seriously needed some sun.

"You okay?"

I looked at Sam. She looked paler than usual and I put a hand to my neck. "Yeah. Apparently so. You ah…did it again."

She nodded and I saw she'd been crying. She sniffed. "Yeah, you're oh for three now."

That didn't make me all that happy. I had to do something so Sam didn't have keep fixing me. She was starting to look tired.

She pushed herself up and reached down to me. "Let's take a look inside. But stay behind Mike, okay?"

I stood. Mike led the way into the mausoleum. It was cramped inside, with very little room for much more than a sideways slide along the sides. Sam created one of those little mini-suns like she had in the other cemetery and sent it up so the light would illuminate the small area.

The center of the space held a coffin on a stand. The top of it came to my waist and it looked new. Along the walls on either side were concrete squares with names and dates engraved on them. The wall opposite the opening was blank, except for a portrait of a man and a woman. A small gold nameplate below it had something etched on it, but I couldn't see it. I figured they were the great grandparents of the family in the tomb.

"You guys ready to lift the lid?" Mike looked at each of us.

"This is creepy." I glanced at the opening where I heard Grey barking outside and I hoped the pentagram holding that Changeling didn't evaporate. I assumed Grey would let us know. "But okay." Mike and I found the hinges and positioned ourselves on the opposite side of the casket while Sam continued holding the light. "One…two… three…"

We lifted the lid.

"Mrs. Jessica Reinhold looks good," Mike said. "So…where's the shroud?"

"Shroud really is a figure of speech," Sam said as she produced a white handled knife. She leaned inside the coffin and cut off a square of the woman's dress.

"That's so wrong," Mike made a face.

"A shroud is historically known as the cloth or linen a body is interned in. Since we dress bodies nowadays and we don't burry them in cloth, this is the closest to a shroud we're gonna get." She pulled a baggie from her back pocket, dropped the square in, closed it, and shoved it back in her pocket.

"That's just…" Mike and I closed the casket. "Kinda anti-climactic."

"Oh I don't know," I led the way out of the mausoleum. "I think near-death is climactic enough for me." My ego was suffering.

Grey guarded the little Changeling. I hadn't really gotten a good look at it since it blitz attacked me. From a distance it was hideous, like a random caricature of what a burned girl would look like. The raincoat was half melted to her body. I glanced over at Mike to see how he was taking it. His jaws were clenched but otherwise I couldn't read him. I looked at Sam. "Can a Changeling create Fae?"

She shrugged. "A Changeling is a type of Fae, but I don't think they can create themselves."

I pointed at the pentagram on the ground holding the creature. "This that spell you were talking about? The one that holds them?"

Sam nodded.

Mike moved to stand next to Grey and faced the Changeling. I wondered how hard it was for him to see the visage of his daughter, burned to a crisp. "How did you know we'd be here?"

"I know what he is. Yes, yes. I know, I know." It pointed past Mike to me. "Guardian, Witch, Sentinel, speaker of spells…." The thing kept repeating the words as if it were rattling off a list. "All those things…so many names it has. But the last…the last is the road that will choose him."

Mike knelt down to its level, his head even with Grey's muzzle. I wasn't sure Mike was paying attention to its little litany. "Your queen sent you here? Was it Medbh? Does she have my daughter, Brendi? The one you were made for?"

The thing stopped muttering and looked at Mike. Well…it really didn't have eyes. More like black sockets. But those sockets could have bored a hole through him. "Brendi. Yes. You are the father. You were the one I was sent to kill." It rushed at Mike but the invisible barrier bounced it back on its ass.

"Yes, I'm Brendi's father." Mike kept his cool, didn't even flinch when the Changeling came at him. "Where is she?"

Brendi Monster moved as close as she could to Mike but kept just out of range of the pentagram's border. "She is Medbh's now. You want her back?"

"Yes."

Sam spoke up. "Mike…don't make a deal with it."

Brendi Monster laughed. "You stay out of this, *Witch*. The father wants the daughter. Then you give me that." She pointed at me.

I made a face; a bit uncomfortable I'd just been made into bargaining chip. I'd prefer we use the mantle.

"Why?" Mike asked. "Why would want Dags?"

But the Changeling just laughed. "Wouldn't you like to know?" It laughed again and I had to wonder how it was even moving. It was little more than a charred skeleton. "He *burrrrrrned* us. You see it? He *burrrrrrned* everything! The queen was angry. So she destroyed it all."

I glanced at Grey. She glanced back at me. I wanted to ask her out loud what she thought, but I assumed she didn't want Mike and Sam knowing she could talk since neither of them seemed to know this. So I tried it another way. *She's not wrong. I did set everything on fire.*

She licked her muzzle. *You did some serious damage to the Cairn. Medbh got mad and punished her. You can see that for yourself.*

"So I didn't do *that*?" I goofed and said it out loud. Grey hung her head.

"Didn't do what, Dags?" Sam stepped forward.

Oh yes, you did the burn damage. Medbh punished her by not letting her die. She's living every second in agony.

Sonofabitch.

This time the Changeling screamed out and charged at me but was stopped again. A flash of blue white light and the thing was popped back against the tree. "*Your* fault…how were we supposed to know you weren't human? Not Witch, but you smell like one. You have such power…"

"What did you tell Medbh?" Mike said.

"Nothing!" the thing shrieked and talked to Mike and I both. "She wouldn't listen! Let me bring him back to her. I show her he isn't right. She used me to see you. She knows you…" it laughed softly, and sounded eerily like a little girl. "But she can't remember you. Magic… so much magic in you…" She reached out with fingers half burned to the bone. "You could fix me."

"Fix you?" Mike glanced back at me and I shrugged.

"He can heal us. I can smell the indecision," she laughed and turned her head toward Sam. "You think the queen is your enemy and yet you work along side…" she turned her eye-less face back to me. "Death."

I backed away. "It's not my fault. You were threatening to touch me with dust. I had to defend myself."

"Four choices! Four roads!" she pointed at me with a finger missing most of its flesh. "I see you now. Hidden inside this man's flesh. You think you can hide from all of them and live as a normal person. The day will come when you will be feared most among all creatures, in all worlds, and no place, no one will give you sanctuary."

"Stop it." I didn't know why her words terrified me, but they did. "Stop saying that."

"Dags—"

The Changeling laughed again. "You will choose the wrong road!"

"No I won't!"

"You already have!"

Mike stood at that moment, pulled his gun from his back pocket and shot the creature in the head. It crumpled to the ground.

"Wait!" Sam moved forward. "We could've kept questioning it."

"It wasn't going to give us anything we need. Brendi's with Medbh. That's all I need to know." He shoved his gun back in his pocket and walked off. Sam shoved her hands into her pockets and followed him. Grey and I watched the body for a few seconds.

"Is she dead?"

Grey came to me and nudged me with her muzzle. *Let's go. You guys have a ritual to perform.*

THE SPELL

We got back to the townhouse just before eleven, making the three-day dead requirement. I jogged upstairs to change out of my now destroyed t-shirt and take a quick shower. I still had blood all over me, even though the wounds were gone. Grey was resting on my bed when I stepped back in from the bathroom.

Who is the woman on the edge of your memories?

After I closed the door, I looked at her. "You can see that?" I rubbed at my hair with a towel.

Yes. Sometimes. When Sam was healing you, I could see her clearly. I felt as I'd seen her before.

"You have?" I moved to the bed. "Where? That was my mother. It's the only clear memory I have of her."

I'm not sure Dags. I just feel as if I know her. Once. You must forgive me. My human memory fails me now and then.

"Why don't you want them to know you can talk? Did you make me forget earlier?"

Yes. I will change your memory again if you try to tell them.

"Why?"

It's not necessary they know I can talk.

I stood in the middle of the room, towel around my waist, one in my hand, talking to a wolf. "You're Fae?"

Laugher in my mind. It tickled. *Hardly. But I am now a part of that world.*

"*Now* a part of it? You weren't before?"

No. I was like you once. A Witch. You're looking at what Medbh does to the Witches she traps and tries to force to do her bidding.

Son of a bitch. "Hunt Beasts."

She put her head down between her outstretched paws. *She has six of us total. But I'm the only one that found my way out of her world.*

I sat on the bed beside her, mindful my towel stayed in place. "Then you know for sure if Brendi's with Medbh, or in a Cairn?"

Grey turned her face away. *I know where she is.*

"She's alive?"

Yes.

"Then why haven't you told those two before? You've been letting them poke around in the dark. Can I tell them if you won't?"

You can't.

"Why all the secrecy? And if I hadn't been in the Cairn and not been able to hear you—"

Then you wouldn't have to keep my secret either.

"The secret that you can talk? That you were human once?"

Finally, she lifted her head and looked at me. And for the first time I saw her eyes weren't that of a wolf's, but a human's. A single tear slid down and she put a paw on my thigh. *You can't tell them, Darren Gregory. If you do, I'll die.*

First, I was surprised she knew my middle name. I rarely ever confessed to that one, be it my dad's name or not. But the dying thing? "I don't understand. How does that work? I mean I know you're not really a wolf. Why can't they?"

Close your eyes.

I did as she asked and felt a pressure in the room. My ears popped and I smelled something sweet, like floral perfume.

Orange blossoms.

"Open your eyes."

That time I heard Grey's voice in my ears and not my mind. I opened them and immediately jumped off the bed because there wasn't a wolf there anymore, but a woman. A naked woman. Her hair was the color of Grey's white undercoat and the roots of it were gray like her upper coat. But the eyes…the eyes told me so much more. This woman was the wolf. "You're…"

"Remember how I said I escaped Medbh's land? I did this by making a bargain with the queen's jailor. He has possession of my true form. What you see before you is only illusion, Darren. I am still a wolf with the mind of a woman."

As if to test this for myself, I reached out and touched her arm. My fingers felt soft fur. "Is this who you were?"

"Yes. But now the jailor keeps my physical likeness in a jar on his shelf. He has many of them in his collection."

"So…how does it work if we tell Sam and Mike…"

"Because that's the price. I can walk in the Human World, interact as a beast, only as long as no one knows my true form. If you tell them I can speak, that I was human, my wolf will shatter like a mirror."

"But *I* know what you are."

"You're not fully human. And you've been inside a Cairn."

I didn't really ignore the comment about my not being fully human. It just wasn't news to me. Hell, the fact I had a physical book inside of me and wasn't dead attested to the fact my physiology wasn't exactly normal by *Grey's Anatomy*. I licked my lips and lowered my hand. "So why Sam and Mike? Why are you hanging around them?"

"Hey Dags! We're ready to get this ritual started!" Sam called up from downstairs. I glanced over at the clock on the nightstand.

I clutched at my towel, waiting on an answer.

The woman looked down and in that gesture I saw it. It wasn't obvious at first, and if I hadn't spent time with Sam, I wouldn't have seen it now. The resemblance nearly took my breath away. "You're Sam's mother."

"Yes."

I put a hand to my face. "Oh hell this sucks. So you can be around your daughter but you can't tell her you're alive?"

"She still believes I died when she was eight. She was such a small child then. I...made an enemy who made a deal with Medbh to get rid of me. This was the queen's solution."

"Won't the queen be mad to know you're here?"

"Do you really think she cares, Darren? The queen is little more than a child herself, a very spoiled child whose station and existence are an afterthought of an idea, born out of a drunken stupor. The queen cares for very little, except for a way to move about in the human world, in our world. It's her obsession. And she believes using a Witch is the only way to make that happen."

"But why?"

"Why? Because in the Other Worlds, you can't feel," she frowned up at me. "Didn't you know this? There is no real physical anything. Emotions are little more than balls tossed about to pass the time. Sensations are merely echoes. But the legends of the things experienced in our world, the material one, are a mighty force, Darren. They're a treasure any creature desires," she smiled. "And so far, the only residents of the Other Worlds who've successfully integrated themselves into our world are the Revenants. But even they have to give up so much of their own power to do this. And giving up power is not something any creature from *Alfheim* is willing to do."

She reached out and touched my arm. It looked like her fingers were moving over my skin, but I felt the pads of a large wolf instead. "This. *Touch*. A simple sensation. And taste. Oh how extraordinary things taste in this world of existence."

"Are you saying there's no sensation associated with touch where she's from? That doesn't make sense. How can there be no sensation? I mean...if Medbh tortures people, don't they feel it?"

"It's hard to explain if you've never been there, or experienced the difference. But to do that you'd have to become half Faerie like me and that's not a curse I'd wish on my worst enemy. Just try and understand that to be here, to be physical, is one of her strongest fantasies," Grey dipped her head. "And the mantle."

I rubbed at my chin.

"Dags?"

"I need pants!" I hollered back and looked at Grey. "So the mantle exists? You mentioned it earlier."

"Yes. And it *is* one of the things the queen wants. Possibly even more than walking here without turning to ash."

"Why's the mantle so important?"

"Oh Darren…have you never been in love?"

Now that was a loaded question. "Not that I remember."

"Love…makes you do really strange things. Medbh loved Oberon above everyone else. When the mantle disappeared just after he pledged his love for Tzariene—Medbh accused Oberon of taking it back and cursed him."

"She cursed the King of the Faeries?"

"Oh yes. She's more powerful than Oberon. She turned him into a donkey. And he was stuck that way for over a century, until Tzariene found the spell to weave him out of it. But he still has some seriously big ears to this day because of it."

I couldn't stop myself from laughing. She laughed as well, and I thought I heard a wolf chuff. We both turned at the sound of someone coming up the stairs and I managed to duck into the closet when the door burst open.

"Dags!" It was Sam.

"Hey, I'm naked!" I grabbed the door of the closet and closed it. My towel fell.

"It's not like I haven't seen it all already, Dags. I took care of you when I first met you."

Oh.

Now that's embarrassing.

"Why's Grey on your bed?"

"We were talking."

"Funny. I'm taking her out for a walk. Be downstairs when I get back."

I listened for the door to shut and then stepped out. I grabbed a pair of clean jeans, another t-shirt and underwear. The socks came on last and I sat on the bed to pull them up. Everything Grey told me *felt* right. It had this unexplainable ding of truth. Truth as far as she knew the truth to be.

Grey was Sam's mother. I didn't know a thing about her mother. I really didn't know a damn thing about Sam.

And I was pretty sure her mom's name wasn't Grey.

With a last look around the room and a double look at my chest and neck in the mirror over the dresser, I jogged down the steps and into the living room.

The place looked…well…witchy was the best word I could come up with. The coffee table became an altar, and on it she'd placed a silver bowl of sand, a red candle, two white candles, a pinecone and a pair of deer antlers. The whole set up looked a little…primitive.

Mike joined me, a beer in his hand. He nodded to the table. "She told me what each represents, but I don't get it. I figured we'd burn a little incense, light a fire and chant."

I gave him a sad face. "You watch way too many movies. I can take a guess at each object's meaning, but every practitioner is different. I can't say what's right and what's wrong."

"You talk like you've had some experience at this."

"I have." I shoved my hands into my pockets. I wanted a beer but figured it was better to keep my head as clear as I could. "So… how much do you know about Sam?"

"Uhm…not a lot. We've sort of gotten to know about each other since we started working together."

"How did that happen?"

"She answered an ad I put in the local psychic rag in Atlanta right before I headed down here. She called about a minute later and got in the car that night. Showed up with a wolf. She's found out more about Brendi's disappearance than anyone else."

"True…but has she ever talked about herself? Like her family?"

"Not really. What little she has shared was just…she's an only child. Mother died when she was eight and her dad raised her."

The wolf made herself comfortable on the sofa after she and Same returned from their walk. Sam joined Mike and I. "Let's get this shit started." Sam pulled the baggie out of her back pocket and placed it on the coffee table. When she went down on her knees, so did Mike and I. Mike on her left and I on her right. I watched her light the altar, seeing a pattern in her movements, as well as seeing the Astral and Mental lights she bent into will. The little colorful orbs appeared again and settled around her. One on her shoulder, one on her arm in the crook of her elbow, and the other two moved about the coffee table altar.

Once the incense was fired up, she took the piece of dress she'd cut out of the baggie and motioned for me to grab the book. I took it off the kitchen table and placed it on the coffee table in front of her. After transcribing it, she'd actually added it to the BBOE like everyone before her. Sam had mad drawing skills and great penmanship.

After she recited the spell in translated English she dropped the piece of cloth on the lit briquette. It ignited almost immediately and sent a burst of purple and white smoke into the air.

The answer was in the smoke and I saw it a second before Sam pointed it out.

She and I both stared at each other when we recognized what and where the mantle was.

Mike didn't see the image in the smoke and looked at each of us. "What? Where is it? Please don't tell me it's in Alaska. I can afford Portland maybe, but I can't fly to Alaska to get it."

"No, it's not in Alaska." Sam waved at the smoke, which had now filled the townhouse. I got up and went to the front window. It lifted easily and the smoke instantly darted out the opening.

"Where?"

"It's here in Savannah," I said as I grabbed a magazine and fanned the smoke in the direction of the window.

"It is? Well that's a stroke of luck," he paused. "So why do you two look like that?"

"Well," Sam said as she sat back on the floor. "It's more of *where* it is that has me puzzled."

"Oh?"

"Tell him, Sam," I said as I rejoined them at the coffee table.

She looked at Mike. "You know that sash Thomas has tied around his top hat?"

Mike nodded, then his eyes widened. "No…"

"Yes," Sam and I said together.

"Thomas the Rhymer has Medbh's mantle."

"'Fraid so. Which means," she said as she looked at me. "We gotta come up with a good thing to trade with him."

Grey yawned on the sofa and smacked her tail on the cushions.

"You don't think he'll give it to us?"

"Dags…what do you know about Thomas the Rhymer?"

"Just what's in the old story about him," I leaned back against the sofa and Grey put a paw on my shoulder. "I know he stumbled or was taken into Fairyland and the queen, whom I assume was Tzariene, allowed him to stay there for a little while. And when she helped him back home, seven years had passed."

"That's the generic version." Sam picked up the candlesnuffer and put out the flames in the reverse order she lit them. "It's true up to a point, but at the time he arrived, Medbh was Oberon's love, and when he was finally released it was because of Tzariene's kindness. I've never gotten the whole story from Thomas or his version. But if he's kept that veil that close to him over the centuries then I'd be more than a little sure it means something to him."

"I would too," Mike said. "And what if he won't give it to us?"

"Then we're back to square one and running out of options."

THE GRiMOiRE

Heading down to River Street at two in the morning seemed crazy to me. But Sam and Mike wanted to tackle getting the mantle from Thomas as soon as possible. Once we had it in our hands—then the fun would begin. I wasn't really looking forward to confronting a Faerie queen. My vote was sleep, *then* we go after her in daylight.

I lost.

Finding Thomas wasn't that hard. He was the only carriage still trolling Bay Street at that hour. He was traveling west when we waved at him from across the street. He waved back, big smiles, turned and pointed to the River Street side and pointed down. I discovered what he pointed to was a scary-as-fuck flight of stairs to River Street and one of the cobblestone driveways that gave access to cars and tourists willing to mutilate their alignment driving on rocks.

Thomas brought his carriage down to meet us and I realized he was the only horse and buggy driver I'd seen do this as long as I'd been in Savannah. Given the whole alignment issue, I wondered if the cobblestone messed with his carriage. I mean, weren't horses and buggies *the* means of transportation when cobblestones covered all the city roads?

Once at the bottom of the stairs, I gave the area a cursory look and realized we were exactly where I'd escaped the Cairn. The thought made me shake and I moved as far away from the retaining wall as I could.

"Ah…I see you remember, Mr. McConnell." Thomas jumped off the carriage and landed gracefully beside it. On the outside he appeared to be a man in his fifties, but on the inside, if this really was *the* Thomas the Rhymer, he was far older than that. "Samantha." He offered his hands to her as he kissed each of her cheeks. Then he offered a hand to Mike. The two shook hands and then embraced. Last he leaned down to offer a hand to Grey. "Ah, Mistress Grey. I see you're looking more lovely than ever."

The wolf offered him her paw and he kissed it. To anyone else that would look really weird. But I assumed he knew the wolf's true form. Thomas straightened and looked at me. "Your colors have shifted, Mr. McConnell. You've tapped a much stronger magic."

I nodded but didn't make any attempt to move closer. Thomas represented a recent traumatic experience and the thought of getting too close to him terrified me.

He looked at everyone. "What brings you down this way so late into the dark time?"

Dark time?

"He means after midnight," Sam filled in the blank as she hooked her thumbs into her jeans. "Thomas, we have a problem." She gave him the short version of what'd happened with the Fae in the cemetery and the ritual we'd performed in the townhouse. Apparently, he already knew about Mike's daughter. When she finished they eyed one another. "I'm guessing…you know what the smoke revealed to us?"

The carriage driver didn't look the least bit surprised. "Yes. I possess the queen's mantle. But I will tell you now, I will not give it up."

Mike stepped toward him. "This is to save my daughter—"

Thomas held up a hand. "I understand that. And having been a prisoner, as well as a guest, in *Alfheim*, I can attest to her plight." He glanced at Grey. I noticed it. Did they? "But the mantle holds a very special place for me."

"You stole it."

"No."

Mike and Sam glanced at one another. "But you have it," Sam ventured.

"The veil is not something Medbh should possess," he said as his expression darkened. "And because you now know its location, I fear others may now discover it."

"We haven't told anyone, Thomas. And we don't plan on it. The information we gleaned said the mantle was a token from Oberon to Medbh. Then it was stolen just as he pledged his love to Tzariene."

He narrowed his eyes at Sam. "The mantle is more than a token, young Witch. It possesses the power to foresee the future."

I arched an eyebrow at him. "In the legend of Thomas the Rhymer, it says the Queen of Faerie gave him a gift of prophecy. You're saying the mantle wasn't stolen but given to you so that you could become a prophet?"

"Not quite. The mantle was never given to Medbh. It was originally given to me. Medbh stole it and held me in her dungeon for several nights before...." again he glanced at Grey. "Before I was rescued. I took the mantle back and returned to this world with the blessings of Oberon. And I have held onto the mantle ever since. You see, she only wants the mantle back so she can know the future."

"But you can't change the future—" Mike began.

"Actually," Sam said, running her fingers through her hair. "I think you can if you can find the linchpin that starts the avalanche of events that nexus into a specific event you can mess with the outcome."

Thomas laughed. "I see you've been reading, Samantha. That's nearly a direct quote from a very old tome...one I've not seen in several decades." He looked at me.

I wondered if he meant the Big Book of Everything because I didn't think she'd been reading the Grimoire without me knowing.

"Thomas, I have to have the mantle. It's the only thing we can think of that she might agree to trade for my daughter," Mike sounded a little upset. Couldn't blame him.

"There is one thing she desires more." He was still looking at me, which made me nervous. I took a step back when Sam and Mike turned to look at me as well.

"What?"

Grey immediately moved to stand in front of me and made a low growl.

Mike looked back at Thomas. "We can't give her the Grimoire… that book can't come out of him."

"It can."

"But won't it kill him?"

"Yes."

"You want us to kill Dags? Me to kill my best friend?"

I swallowed and held my hands out to my sides. I swore if any of them came at me ready to carve this book out of my insides I was going to make my own little fire party.

"No," the carriage driver shook his head. "You see…what even the Guardian doesn't know, is that if the book is taken from him forcefully, if his life is destroyed in the process of removing it, then the book will be destroyed as well."

I blinked. "What? I thought it would be up for grabs."

"No one's told you, have they? Not even the Angel that follows you. Haven't you wondered why the Choirs of the Light World—if they wanted that book so bad—haven't simply killed you and taken it? They have the knowledge to do it. They could make you a Power, a willing servant of their cause, one of the faithful, but no such gesture has been made. Because they know, all of them know, if you die the book vanishes. It becomes a part of the Well of Souls, and the knowledge is disseminated into the psyche of the universe once again."

I felt like I'd just received a very important piece of knowledge. I just wasn't getting it.

Sam and Mike had very similar confused looks on their faces. "What in the hell are you talking about?" Sam looked back at Thomas. "You mean the knowledge in that book, its power, would become a part of the Souls?"

"Yes. So you see why no one wants this boy killed as much as…

held. Bound to them," he shook his head and his expression was sad. "There is a fight for him. A fight that is carried out in the shadows. Powerful individuals plot to find way of binding him to them. If they control him, they control a mighty power."

I waved at him dismissively. "Wait…stop. No one's binding me or controlling me. But I do want to get back to the *can't be killed* part?"

"What would you like to know?"

"What about old age? Dying of natural causes? Heart attack?"

"Guardian, what happened in Bonaventure? When the Changeling wrought upon you more damage than any normal human could survive? You didn't see it but they did," he nodded to Mike and Sam. "She ripped your throat out."

"How do you know this?" Mike said.

Sam touched his arm. "He's a prophet. He probably saw it before it happened."

I glanced at Mike and Sam. Neither of them had told me exactly what the Changeling did. I wasn't sure I wanted to know. "The book came out of me—"

"Holy shit," Sam said, seeming to suddenly understand something I didn't. "You mean if something like that happens to him, that book is going to fix him?"

"Either by its own means or by another's hand. You were there, Samantha Hawthorne, daughter of the Hawthornes of Salem. It recognized you as being of the blood of the God Mother and gave you the spell. But can you remember any of it?"

"No, it was in another language."

"Ah, but your name is in that book now, as is everyone who's ever touched it," Thomas stepped toward me. "I do not believe Medbh realizes the book exists *inside* of a Witch, Guardian. And it would be a bad thing if she ever did."

"I think I know the why on that, but maybe we should hear it?" I said.

"The moment she discovers its existence is the moment your freedom would cease to be. She would hunt you down to use you and the Grimoire to her advantage. Any of the powerful denizens of her world would do the same. *Alfheim* is a dangerous place for you."

I honestly didn't see how that was any different than anyone else wanting the book, so I said as much.

"The Choirs play by the rules, those of…*Alfheim*, do not. I could tell Medbh to her face if she destroyed you to get to the book, the book would vanish and she would never believe me. Even with proof. You must keep the knowledge of that book secret from her."

Add another idiot to the list of the cray-cray.

Sam spoke up. "But Thomas…she had Dags as a prisoner in that Cairn. You're telling us she can't *see* the Grimoire?"

"The Grimoire doesn't exist in that world, not in a form that's visible to her. In the Cairn she couldn't see it. It's part of the Astral World but with a demonic beginning. Once it moves into *Alfheim*, then it is possible for her to see it, unless its power is masked," he looked at me in a thoughtful position, pulling at his beard with his fingers.

"How do you know all of this?" Mike asked. "I mean, you seem to know more about that book than Dags, and it's in his soul."

Thomas reached up and touched the cloth wrapped around his hat. "I can see the future, the past and the present. They're not always clear but I can see the Guardian with two women and know it is a past vision," his filmy eyes unfocused for a second. "I cannot give you the mantle, Michael. But I can put it where it will be well protected."

Thomas removed his top hat. "Yes. Things are in flux now. Times are changing, becoming more mysterious as walls break, alliances crumble and old enemies wake in the dark," he untied the mantle from the hat, replaced the hat on his head and meticulously folded the mantle as he spoke. "Using the mantle to trade for another life is tantamount to asking Armageddon if it would like to come over for tea and then being surprised that it mounted your cat and escaped through the pet door." He finished folding the mantle until it was perfectly flat. Abruptly it sparkled red and disappeared and then a piece of paper reappeared.

In fact, the paper looked like one of the pages of the Grimoire—

I wasn't ready or prepared for what Thomas did next. Neither was

Sam or Mike. The prophet lunged toward me and thrust his fist and the piece of paper into my chest. I mean literally *into* my chest. His hand disappeared up to his wrist inside of me. The sensation wasn't painful, but it wasn't pleasant either. It was like getting a tooth filled on painkiller. I knew someone was inside of me, rummaging around and it was uncomfortable, and I knew on some level the pain was going to come later. And as long as his hand was in there I couldn't move.

Sam gasped and Mike lunged at Thomas. But the prophet held up his other hand and Mike stopped moving. For a brief moment—*everything* stopped moving, except for Thomas.

And Grey. She appeared in her human form.

"Darren, we've only got seconds so you have to listen to me." It was Thomas's words, but Grey's voice. They both glowed where they stood and I felt nauseous. "Medbh cannot, under any circumstances, have this mantle. So it must remain with you, inside the book where it will be protected. The mantle will mask the power of the Grimoire while in *Alfheim*, but Thomas has no idea how long. Medbh could see through the rouse at any time."

"But we have to get Brendi—"

"The Grimoire has a spell that will duplicate the mantle, but the magic of it will only last a short time. If she tries to use the mantle, it'll evaporate into little more than dust. The veil is now in the book so the book knows what to do."

The slight pause alarmed me. "But?"

"In order to create the fake, you'll need Faerie dust. The real stuff."

"And where do I get that?"

They both looked behind me at the retaining wall. I glanced back and saw the scorched entrance I'd left behind that day. "No...no I can't go back in there. You don't understand...I can't—"

"Darren, you have to get over that fear. Take Sam and Mike with you—"

"But I can't do that," my face twisted into an angry grimace. "You forget how sick I was when I came out of that place? If they go in with me we'll all come out in need of a hospital."

"Sam and Mike *can* go with you. If you use the Grimoire to protect them."

"I can do that?" This was news to me.

"Yes. It'll protect them but I'm afraid it'll also drain a good deal of your energy. So you'll have get in and get out. Also, you can't allow any of the dust to touch them. Nor can you allow any of the creatures trapped there to notice you. Once they do, Medbh will know you're there and then it'll be up to you to get all three of you out."

I didn't like the sound of any of this. Why couldn't things just work the way they're supposed to? Just...get the mantle, get the kid and have pizza?

"Darren, you're right that the only thing that'll make her part with one of her little Witches is this mantle. But we can't—"

"I know, I know. I just..." I didn't want to go back in there.

"Is Brendi worth it?"

I looked back at Grey even though Thomas was talking. "Yes. She is."

"Just remember one thing," Grey reached out to me and touched my cheek. "Upon returning the mantle to Medbh, she will grant you a wish. When it's time to make the wish, *you* must make it. And no one else. But you must wait to use it."

The scene abruptly vanished as if someone turned off a switch. I landed on my ass and Sam dove down next to me. She pushed me onto my back and looked at my chest, pulled my t-shirt up to see my skin. "Hey!" I protested.

Well, I didn't protest *emphatically*.

"What the fuck did you do old man?" Mike had his gun out and pointed at Thomas.

Grey came up and nuzzled Mike's crotch, promptly diffusing the situation.

Sam looked at me and then up at Mike. "What the fuck just happened? Where's the damned mantle?"

I pushed at her to let go of me and both of us stood up. This time I dusted myself off before I spoke. It gave me a few minutes to figure out what to say. "I have the mantle. It's in the Grimoire."

"What?" Mike had the word out of his mouth no sooner than something exploded between us.

He flew backwards and rolled along the cobblestone drive. Sam was blasted back and struck the retaining wall where the Cairn opening had been. She slumped on the ground and remained very still. Grey growled and yapped as she charged at me—

No. At *us*. I hadn't been blasted because the Changeling—or what had once been a Changeling and was now a rotting zombie—had appeared and grabbed me, her hand around my neck. It was the cemetery all over again as my feet dangled above the ground and I held onto her boney, slimy wrists. I tried to warn Grey not to bite the mean Changeling, but couldn't speak. Hell, I couldn't breathe.

Grey charged at the Changeling, but the thing kicked at her. She cried out and rolled away. When she didn't get back up I tried kicking the thing.

That just made her tighten her grip. She turned her attention back to me. "Mine, Witch. Guardian. Give me the mantle." She had me with one hand and now tore at my front with her other. I had a pretty good idea she'd seen Thomas shove it into my chest and she was going after it. "I will have it. Medbh will grant my wish!"

"I'm afraid you already know that's impossible," Thomas's voice was calm and even. Whatever blast the Changeling had used for her entrance hadn't fazed him. He stood exactly where he'd been before. "As a Fae, Medbh will not grant you a wish."

She dropped me as she turned to face Thomas. I half landed on my feet but my ankle twisted painfully and I grabbed it with both hands. It took a few seconds for the agony to dim and I half lay on my left side, my right foot in my hands. I glanced over my shoulder but couldn't see where Mike ended up. Sam and Grey remained still as stone.

"Now just who are you?"

Thomas clasped his hands in front of him. "What do your burned out eyes tell you?"

I tried moving away from the two of them but standing wasn't possible. At least not yet. I was pretty sure the ankle wasn't broken, maybe sprained. Running—totally not happening. Crawling was an option so I began a very long, painful (over cobblestone!) crawl toward Sam and Grey.

"You're just a human. An old, weak man."

"I have lived in this world for over a century, Changeling," Thomas said as he lifted his right hand and pointed up with his index finger. "You will not harm me."

"You *lie*."

The Changeling didn't sound completely convinced of her own accusation. She took another step back and turned to look at me. I froze and braced myself for another attack. But she just pointed at me and looked at Thomas. "That *Witch* possesses the mantle, the one thing Medbh wants more than all the kingdoms in all the worlds."

"Yes?" Thomas sounded surprised. "And you cannot have it, my useless friend."

Sam made a noise to my right and I split my attention from crawling to her and listening to the two of them.

The Changeling drew herself up. "You're trying to trick me. Deceive me. Trap my attention so the little man can get away," she turned toward me.

A sword appeared in my hand. Positioned between the Changeling and Sam and Grey, I held the sword up. So much crazy shit had been happening to me—I didn't even question it. "Back off, ugly."

"Calm down," Thomas's voice was calm. "If you become angry, the book will act—"

"Shut. Up!" I saw an image of fire. A lot of fire. So much of it that it engulfed everything. And for a brief few seconds, I wanted it to. I wanted to burn the entire city, all of Savannah. I wanted it blessed and purged by fire!

Abruptly, small fires flared all around us. Pockets of flame burned on the stairs, the wall and the ground.

Thomas's buggy caught on fire.

I caught Sam moving out of the corner of my eye and breathed as sigh of relief. A quick glance at her and she was getting to her feet beside a slowly moving Grey.

The Changeling moved toward the retaining wall and picked up a pipe. I didn't know how to fight with a sword, not really. But muscles I didn't realize I had moved and within seconds she and I were fighting. She thrust, I parried. She swung, I blocked. The first few seconds were her attacking and me defending. I was pretty sure the skeletal Changeling and I looked like a scene right out of *Jason and the Argonauts.*

Until... *"Batiltu!"*

The Sumerian word for stop came out of my mouth before I knew it, and to my surprise, the Changeling froze in mid swing. Everything about her stopped. All movement. It was like looking at a movie still.

I lowered the sword and stumbled back into Sam's arms. She reached around me with her right hand and put it on my forehead. The left hand she brought up under my left arm and pressed against my chest. The fire inside me instantly died. My anger, my resentment, my rage. It all sizzled away into nothing as she took the sword and threw it.

I thought she was getting rid of it, until I saw Mike appear. He caught it with both hands, turned and swung it at the Changeling, removing its head. The bones crumpled in a heap to the ground.

The sword vanished and I almost collapsed against her. "Shh..." she said in my ear. "I won't let her hurt you again."

You know...I was still waiting for the day *I* could tell a woman that.

A NEW PAGE iN THE BOOK

Mike kicked at the bones as he ran to the buggy and helped Thomas put the fire out. Blood flowed in small rivulets down the left side of his face and he had dirt on his cheek, but he looked good. Once the buggy wasn't flaming, he immediately came to me and put his hands on my shoulders as Sam released me. "We really need to have a talk about you and using fire. You could have burned us all."

"I can't control it."

"Mike. Don't. He's still tapping the power. I'm pretty sure when you started fighting you got your ass kicked. A lot. Before you knew what you were doing."

I managed to stand on my own, but I wasn't happy with the look Mike was giving me. I knew he was stressed about Brendi, and every time I was around, something went wrong and delayed us that much more from finding her.

"The Grimoire protects," Thomas said as he stepped back from his buggy.

I moved away from Sam on wobbly legs toward him. "Thomas—about your buggy—"

"Oh, you'll buy me a new one, Mr. McConnell. But first, you have dust to find."

I was going to offer to get it fixed. That I could swing. But buying him a new one? I didn't have unlimited funds. But it had been my magic that toasted his source of income. I turned and looked at Sam. One side of her face was darker than the other, but I didn't know if that was a bruise or dirt. I also had to ask myself, if she grabbed me from the front where I could see her instead of from the back, would I have tried to hurt her? Would I have burned her?

Sam dusted herself off. Grey sat at her feet, wagging her tail. "So we need dust to make the mantle. That means we have to go into the Cairn, right?"

I looked past her to the retaining wall. The grate entrance was there. "Does anyone else see that?"

Sam turned.

"When the hell did they put that drainage grate in there?" Mike asked as he stepped up beside me.

"That's not a real drainage grate," I said. "That's the Cairn." When they turned and looked at me, wide-eyed, I shrugged. "That's what I came out of."

Sam wrapped her arms around her chest and started pacing. I thought she was chanting something, until she passed close by me and what I heard was, "Shit, shit, shit, shit…"

I was really starting to like her.

Mike didn't seem as upset. I could tell he was ready to jump in and do his part. He wanted his little girl back.

But me…I wasn't ready to put them at risk. I was carrying a book of spells with the firepower of a flamethrower. And I'd actually stopped a Changeling in its tracks without thinking. Was the magic capable of doing what I wanted with just a word? I held out my hand and thought pizza.

Nope.

"You'll need to be careful going through the Cairn. Medbh's spies will be everywhere."

"Spies?" Mike said.

Sam stopped pacing. "Could be anything. Rats, spiders, roaches. Anything Medbh can use as her eyes and ears in the Cairn. Just like she'd used that Changeling."

That didn't sit well with me. "Right. So…let me go in there and get the dust and then—"

"No," Sam and Mike spoke in unison.

I lowered my head. "Guys, it's too dangerous. I didn't run that far to get to this exit, so she couldn't have had me too far in. She spilled dust so I can just run in, grab some there."

"Dags," Sam said and had a peculiar frown on her face. "Cairns don't work like that. They don't stay the same. What you walked out of you won't necessarily walk into."

"I'm not following."

"The Fae can't build Cairns, only the Faerie denizens can. But the Fae can manipulate them. That means they have absolute power over those places. Their whims manipulate the texture and landscape. The Changeling probably made it look like a place based on what she believed would disturb you. And it did. It shook you. But what's behind that grate now…." she shrugged. "Could be anything from a volcanic landscape to a butterfly meadow."

Oh. Great. "I'm going to need to protect the two of you if you go in with me."

"Protect us?" Mike holstered his gun.

"From the sickness. Remember that?"

Mike slowly nodded. "You were sick when you came out of there. Would that same thing happen to us?"

Sam answered. "I'm afraid so. Dags you know how to do that?"

"I'm going to have to just trust the book." I closed my eyes and saw the book in my mind and I asked it for a protection spell for them. Instantly, the book opened and the pages turned. I held out my hands. Sam took one and Mike took the other. "*Nasaru*."

Warmth coursed from somewhere in my chest outward, through my arms and into my hands. Sam and Mike's grip tightened and within seconds they both yanked their hands away.

"Oh Sweet Lady…my ears popped," Sam muttered. When I opened my eyes she had her fingers stuck in her ears. If I looked harder at her I could see something twinkling around her and around Mike. I knew on some instinctual level that energy came from me and as long as the spell held, I would find them and keep them close. I wasn't about to tell them they sparkled.

"All right, we need to go in, grab the dust and get out," I looked at each of them.

Sam finally stopped messing with her ears. "No fire."

"I promise."

"Mike, how many rounds you got?"

"Two magazines in my pocket. And I have two knives. They're both steel."

"And the bullets?"

"Steel."

"Good. That'll hurt anything that comes at us, Fae or otherwise."

I glanced at Mike then Sam. "Steel? I thought Faeries couldn't stand iron?"

"What do you think steel's made of?" Sam gave me an odd look as she bent down and pulled a really long knife out of the side of her boot. "Steel's an alloy of iron and carbon."

I would have known that if I hadn't had my eggs scrambled watching her bend over like that. Was it wrong of me to see that as an extremely seductive gesture?

"It won't kill 'em the way straight up iron will," Mike came up beside me and showed me his magazine of bullets. "But it'll hurt them and it makes a really big hole that burns."

Oookay.

Mike slipped the magazine back in his pocket and Sam secured her knife to her belt. "I've got a few bottles in my little pouch, full of a few spells that will buy us time," she patted the fanny pack I'd noticed before. She looked at me. "And we know you've got the flaming sword of doom. You think you can make that thing appear again?"

"I don't think we're prepared to do this right now," Sam started toward the grate. "In fact I don't think we're even close to ready. But I have the feeling the Cairn entrance will be visible for a limited time and if we don't use it now, then we might not get another chance to get the dust."

If she had that feeling, so did I. The fact I hadn't seen it after I fell out of it and now it was visible again confirmed it for me. Going in there needed planning, strategy and a bit of luck. We hadn't planned on a walk through a Faerie Cairn, the only strategy we had was grab the dust and get out if we're lucky. And with recent events, I was pretty sure luck hated me.

We stood in front of the grate and faced it. I did not want to go in there.

"How are we going to carry the dust out?" Mike asked. "If we touch it…doesn't that mean we'll get stuck in there? Or worse we'll end up as obedient zombies to Medbh?"

I turned and looked back at Grey. She hadn't moved from her spot, except to watch us. I didn't ask her a question, not in my head or aloud. I assumed she had an answer.

No, I'm not going. Use your strengths, Darren. And protect my daughter.

That's it?

I'm not kidding. You have potential. You just need to be confident you can use it when the time comes.

I gave her a seriously irritated look and faced the grate. "We improvise."

"Figures," Mike said as he stepped forward, grabbed two thick bars of the grate, and pushed the entire door inward. It made the worst god-awful grinding noise I'd ever heard.

The scent of decay and the acrid hint of something burnt greeted us on a soft breeze.

He gave me a withering look. "I forgot how you usually make this shit up as you go along."

DELiLAH

Mike went in first, then me, then Sam. Grey remained outside, having given me the best excuse not to go.

I escaped from there. Why in the hell would I want to go back in?

True dat.

Unfortunately for me the further in we went, the more likely I would hyperventilate. I was freak'n terrified and kept my arms and legs firmly tucked into the bus. The closer we got to where I thought I was held, the more concentrated the charred smell became.

"Dags…does this look like it did when you were here?"

"Yeah." Our voices echoed against the walls. "It's exactly the same."

She didn't say anything.

"Why do you ask?" I asked.

Sam still didn't answer me and her silence just set off a dozen more internal alarms on the doom meter for me. When the Changeling took me here, I couldn't see where the light had come from. But now it flickered and danced over shadows from lit torches along the rounded sides. The further we went, the dimmer those torches became until they were burned to a crisp. I could make out what remained of their stands, oddly deformed fingers that jutted out from the side.

The only light we had was what came in behind us and elongated our shadows. I did notice how the light coming in, once we were inside, would lead anyone to believe the sun was bright in the human world. When in truth I knew it was closer to three in the morning.

After a few minutes, we reached the crossroads where I'd been tied to a chair. There wasn't a chair or the ropes left. There was something else missing as well.

"Dags…I thought you said there were piles of Faerie dust here…" Sam moved along the side. She held out her hand, blew into her palm and a blue and white light appeared in the center, about the size of an orange. She tossed it into the air where it stopped just below the dark, scorched ceiling and expanded into a flat disk. The diffused light illuminated the entire area. It wasn't as bright as the mini-sun she'd used before and reminded me of moonlight. "Because I don't see any."

I moved around in a circle, giving the floor a much harder look. "Neither do I."

"You sure this is where you were held?" Mike moved opposite of Sam and then looked at me.

There wasn't anything discernible about this particular junction. Nothing on the walls, or the floor, that told me this was *the* spot where I'd been tied up. The memory was still hazy from waking up and being disoriented at the time. The only clear memories I had were of pain, fear and running the hell away. I stood in the center and tried to remember if I'd turned left or right on my flight out of the Cairn.

"Shit," Sam said in a low voice after watching me. "You can't remember can you?"

"No," I held out my hands. "Sorry for being freak'n scared out of my mind. I wasn't mapping out the tunnels in case I needed to return. I planned on never showing my face here again."

"Well, you said you could see the light at the end of the tunnel from where you were tied up, right? So I say we keep moving away from the light and we might hit another one of these junctions."

"Uh…Sam," Mike had moved away from us to the tunnel on our left. I could see him several feet in. "You gotta see this."

I followed Sam to the left into the tunnel. He motioned for us to turn around—and when we did, we were looking down the tunnel we'd just entered in front of the light. Physics wasn't one of my strong points, but I knew the basics of position. I knew that if you turned left off a hallway, when you looked back, you'd either see a blank wall which would be the opposite wall of that hallway, or you'd see whatever had been facing the left turn. In this case, we should have been looking at the right-branching tunnel. Or in this case, I should have been able to see the cross tunnel with Sam's little moon suspended in the air.

But I didn't. I saw a tunnel. Period.

"This sucks." Sam moved toward the light and abruptly disappeared.

"Sam?" Mike jogged forward just as her upper half popped up on the right side of the tunnel.

"Yeah?"

He stopped. "Are you in the tunnel we came in?"

"I think. Come toward me."

We both walked toward her and I was sure we turned right, heading back out of the tunnel—

But it never felt as if we'd actually turned right. As one we turned back, with the tunnel's end behind us, and faced three branching tunnels.

"This is fucked up. If we head down any one of these tunnels, we're going to lose track of where we've been because where we've been doesn't look like where we think we've been."

The sentence didn't make a hell of a lot of sense on its own but I understood what he was getting at. I ran a hand through my hair and pulled it off my forehead. This was bad. No, it was worse than bad. But now I understood the legends about people saying they got lost in Faerie. Hell, I doubted they ever made it to Faerie itself 'cause they got lost in the Cairn.

Mike held up his gun. "We've got to check down one of these tunnels and find some dust."

I looked down each of the other three tunnels. The fastest way to do this was to split up and cover each tunnel at the same time. But that also meant isolating each of us, which put each of us at greater danger and unless we could be sure of the direction we were going, then all three of us could get lost. The spell I'd commanded was only meant to guard from the influence of this place, not shield from any kind of attack.

And though there was nothing obvious I could see that would attack us, I didn't want to take chances.

"I know what you're thinking," Sam said. "And the answer is no."

"We can't split up," I turned to her. "Not all three of us. It's too dangerous."

"That might be, but you should take a look at yourself. You're paler now than when we walked in here. I see dark circles under your eyes and you're moving a bit slow. You keeping us protected is taking a toll on you. We gotta do this quick." She held her knife in her hand. "You stay here with Mike while I check a hundred steps down that left tunnel. After a hundred steps, I'll turn around and walk a hundred steps back. When I do, I should bump into you even though it looks like I'm heading down the tunnel."

"Right, and we'll still be able to see you, like we did before."

I nodded with Mike. Sounded like a good plan, but I wanted to do the exploring. I was immediately voted off the island and Mike told me to sit and rest. I sat up against the wall entrance to the left tunnel when Sam started out. Mike and I watched her, and waited, and then just as she became a shadow in the distance, she started getting bigger again until she turned the corner and nearly ran over me. "Oh! That's so weird that you're there and I can't see you."

"Mmhmm," I stood up and brushed myself off. "No dust?"

"None. It's like it was swept clean. Mike, you take the right tunnel and I'll stay here with Dags."

We repeated the process with Mike and after he scratched his head. "No dust. Not even dirt. Just…burned tunnels."

I was starting to think maybe I'd burned the dust up as well as the Cairn. It was decided we'd all move forward, but we'd also leave one of Mike's copper pennies in the middle of the junction so we'd know that was the right way out.

The tunnel stretched out for what seemed like miles into the dark.

And keeping my guard up for a long extended amount of time was exhausting. A few times I got a little dizzy.

"This isn't working. I say we go back, make sure we don't get sick and then summon a little Fae creature and shake the dust off of them. I'm thinking we can trap a Fae easy enough," Sam said. "We could walk around for days in here. There's got to be a map or something."

"I wouldn't think so if Dags burned out this Cairn, which is what it looks like," Mike looked up and around us. "My worry is, I think I'm seeing the exact same scorch pattern."

"What do you mean?" I didn't like that sound of that.

"Well, when I was a kid I used to imagine seeing faces in wood grain, or in concrete in the sidewalk, so I noticed patterns. And since we've been walking together, I've seen the *same* pattern repeat itself."

"What?" Sam turned to face Mike and her eyes widened. "Oh fuck."

I turned around as well to look at Mike, but my eyes slid off his shoulder and refocused on the tunnel behind him. Only there wasn't a tunnel anymore because it was pitch black. "Oh that's not good."

Mike glanced back and his shoulders slumped. "Oh damn."

"We need to get out of here." I moved quickly past him in the direction of where that light *should* be. I was seriously panicking. All those fears of being confined and tortured by a possessed Brendi Monster were scratching at the edges of my sanity. I heard their running footfalls behind me as we made our way down the tunnel, back the way we came.

But the further we traveled, the darker the end of that tunnel grew. Finally, I stopped and they stopped behind me. It was light where we were, but behind us or in front of us was dark. "I..." I was way out of breath. "I...got a...really bad feeling..."

"No shit..." Sam panted to my right. She looked around. "So where is the light coming from? How is it we can see only where we are?"

"Maybe it's like the outer circle of Hell, like in Dante's 'Inferno,'" Mike said, breathing heavily but barely breaking a sweat. "You know, where the souls that never knew God ended up—only it was dark except where they were because their intellect was what lighted the way?"

Sam and I stared at him.

He shrugged. "Sorry. It was just a thought," Mike looked around us. "Shouldn't we be seeing that little moon you made? I know we ran further than we walked, which means we should have found it."

This was bad. Badder than bad. I held out my hands. "If Mike saw repeating scorch marks, that means something like repeating textures, right? Or a repeating scene. Kind of like the old cartoons with the stock backgrounds? When the character ran and the scenery behind continued to repeat the same house and store?"

Mike smirked. "Yeah. It's freaky that you and I had the same thought."

"You make some really weird analogies sometimes, Dags." Sam slipped her knife back into her belt.

"Yeah…I know. But that's not the problem. Either the Cairn is keeping us in the same area or something else is."

We looked at each other and caught our breath.

"Dags…you're looking thin," Mike put a hand on my shoulder.

"I feel it. We've got to get out of here."

He nodded. "We can find some other way to get dust."

"You want dust?" A melodic and somewhat sensual voice said from above us.

Mike's gun was in his hand, Sam's dagger was up and me—well I had my hands up into fists ready to fight whatever or whoever that was. I didn't think I'd win the fight, but I would go down swinging. I just didn't want to set fire to anything else while we were trapped in here.

None of us said anything. I assumed we were too afraid to answer. I was sure they were thinking the same thing I was—this voice belonged to one of Medbh's spies and our cover was blown.

Then, "I know you can hear me."

I looked at Sam and glared. She narrowed her eyes at me as if to say *I'm not gonna answer!* I cleared my throat but it was Mike that spoke and I cringed, thinking this was it. Medbh was going to know we were there we were going to spend our lives as Hunt Beasts. "We're not happy about talking to a voice with no form. Care to show us where you are, and tell us who you are?"

"You promise not to kill me?"

Sam did talk this time. "If you promise not to tell Medbh we're here."

Something moved in the shadows behind Mike. No…actually the *shadows* moved behind Mike. Sam and I saw it at the same time and she grabbed his belt loop and hauled him closer to her.

The shadows clinging to the wall, the ones making the scorch marks we'd seen, oozed and dripped, rose and then culminated into a pile in the middle of the tunnel. The walls no longer looked as if they'd been through a fire. In fact they looked like dirt, as if the tunnel had been hollowed out under ground. Roots, flowers and several underground springs appeared where the black smut had clung.

The burn had all been a lie?

"I don't tell that bitch anything. Not after what she did to this place."

"Oh god, we're not in Kansas anymore," Sam muttered and pulled the two of us to her. Mike on her right and me on her left.

The black smut was both liquid and smoke as it moved and shimmered and formed itself into a seven-foot column. Then the column broke off four appendages that formed into arms and legs. The torso formed and then a head. Black smoke covered it one last time and when it finally cleared, we were looking up at the tallest drag queen I'd ever set my eyes upon.

It was both male and female, with arms like Mike's and a face very similar to Sam's. The breasts were perfectly rounded with just the right amount of perk and the hips and legs were thin like Mike's but rounded like Sam's. The hair was black, as were its eyes and lips. The skin shimmered a ghastly white and when it smiled its teeth looked a lot like the Brendi Monster's. All pointy and sharp.

"Is this better?" its voice was deep and very manly.

Yeah…drag queen.

Mike cleared his throat. "And…who do we have the pleasure of addressing?"

He/she's smile widened as he/she leaned against the wall, closer to Mike. "You are a charmer…and so deliciously…*human*."

"Thank you," Mike's tone remained firm. Calm. But I saw his hand holding the gun shake. "Do you have a name?"

"You must know a name is a gift of power to the other," she pursed her black lips. "So I will give you mine if you give me yours."

Oh no…I tried to mentally warn Mike not to give it his real name! So when he opened his mouth and spoke I was pleasantly surprised. "My name's Leonard. Leonard Nimoy."

She arched a black eyebrow. "That's not your *real* name, is it?"

Mike gave her a pitiful look. "You think I'd choose to be called Leonard?"

When she laughed the floor beneath me vibrated. "True. Then you can call me Delilah."

Drag name. Oy.

"You didn't want *our* names?" Sam asked. I nudged her. Why the hell would she ask that? The thing didn't seem to see us. In fact, I don't think it even looked at us.

When it did, its eyes burned red and it snarled. "No. You stink of the God Mother, blasphemer and betrayer. Your blood is polluted and foul. But the human's…his is pure and strong."

Blood? What sort of Fae creature liked human blood?

Oh god…I hoped like hell we weren't talking about a Fae Vampire, because that was just…fifty shades of wrong.

"I can hear your contempt for me and our kind in your voice, Mother's child. You even speak of yourself in the third person. Believe you are royalty."

Sam opened her mouth for a verbal tirade, but I pulled at her arm and leaned in to whisper in her ear. "I don't think she can see me."

She stared at me and then, "Delilah, how many of us do you see?"

The creature laughed. "You see? You still call yourself us—"

"No, I mean do you see us as only two?" she pointed between herself and Mike.

Delilah frowned. "Of course. What sort of idiotic questions are these?" she turned her attention back to Mike. "I can give you dust if that's what you want...but what will you give me?"

"Hey Delilah!" I shouted at her. My voice echoed in the tunnel, but the tall woman/man didn't look at me. "You're the ugliest queen in the realm and your shoes don't match your pants!"

Still no response. That was just odd. What kind of Fae creature didn't see me but lusted after humans and disliked Witches? I wasn't about to consult the Grimoire. Didn't want to bring attention to myself. "Hey Mike, keep it going. She doesn't see me. We might make this work for us."

He didn't respond and kept a healthy distance between himself and Delilah. "What is it you want in trade?"

"Oh," she reached out to stroke his cheek with a hand the size of his head. Mike stepped away and she looked like she was pouting. "Oh...you reject me already?"

"No...I just need to know what you want in trade. The dust is very important to me."

"But if you touch this dust..." the pout became a grin. "Then you'll be trapped here."

"I know. But that can't happen. I really need the dust."

"Then I will make it easy for you," she turned and looked directly at me. "I want that."

THE SPiDERWYCK'S WEB

I put a hand to my chest. "Me? You can see me?"

Delilah didn't answer. Instead she looked at Mike.

Sam looked from me to Delilah and back to me. "Delilah…what did you point at?"

"I don't know. I can sense it. I can smell its magic. But I can't touch it," she slid a devious look to Sam. "Therefore I know I want it. And I want it before Medbh realizes it's here."

Mike slowly shook his head. "I don't have the power to give whatever it is you sense. I'm afraid my friend and I don't control such things."

Delilah glanced over in my direction. "Pity. At least with me, whatever it is has a chance to survive." She moved from where she'd slumped beside Mike and slid to where I stood. I took several steps back as her black eyes searched the area. From the unfocused look in her eyes, I knew she really couldn't see me. She sniffed…and then sniffed again. "It's here. And it feels…." abruptly she straightened up and oozed back. "Familiar. I've smelled that before. It smells of the fire…"

Uh oh. That didn't sound good.

"Fire?" Sam move to stand just a little in front of me. "What fire? We thought the scorch on the walls was the fire, but that turned out to be you."

"Yesss..." she refocused on Sam. "Because the magic of that fire coats everything. Medbh said it was tainted. Powerful," she hissed. "Etheeeeeereal..."

The fire had been...Ethereal? That didn't make any sense. Unless the spell I'd used from the Grimoire was Ethereal in origin?

"What do you mean by that?" Sam was looking for answers.

But Delilah's form shifted, parts of her legs oozing back into a large puddle of black ocher. "A Changeling brought a prize to us, but it wouldn't share. Wanted to keep it for herself. Believed it was important. Told us Medbh would want it..." Abruptly her eyes become the size of white painted grapefruit. Her mouth extended out to either side in a weird-ass caricature of a well-known DC Comic villain. "But it burned us...it burned everything...and Medbh...*ABANDONED US HERE!*"

Time to go!

All three of us took off running in the opposite direction. I was already tired and this was not helping. I stupidly glanced back to see if she was following, only to behold her ass end changing into the shape of a seven-foot black widow spider. Alongside her ran hundreds of smaller versions, all in hot pursuit of...*us*.

I didn't know how far we'd gone before my side started to hurt. My mom used to say the bear got me when I would run and get this kind of pain. But somehow I was pretty sure this wasn't a metaphorical bear, but a signal I was losing a lot of energy really fast. The spell to guard the two of them, as well as myself, was in super-protect mode. It didn't help that my legs felt like I'd tied iron weights to my ankles. I was lagging behind the two of them and that big ass spider was catching up.

The really stupid idea of refocusing the guarding spell on just the two of them and not myself came to me. I'd already been in the Cairn and survived the illness of re-entry into the Physical World. So without stopping, I imagined lopping off that extension. It worked because the pain in my side disappeared and the weights on my legs lessened.

"Dags! Set it on fire!"

"No! I'm not risking...that. I might burn us too!"

"Then freeze it!"

"No!"

"Here!" Sam shouted and disappeared up ahead on the right. Mike did the same at the same spot, so when I got to that same spot I turned right—and smashed into the wall. The combination of my speed and a sudden stop resulted in me bouncing off the wall and rolling several feet, ass over end, on down the tunnel.

I'd barely come to a stop when something wet and warm grabbed my right ankle. I was on my stomach, every bone and muscle in my body protesting the spill I'd just taken, so I had to twist to see what had a hold of me.

Delilah the spider bore down on me, her upper half a nasty combination of the goth drag queen and the body of an arachnid. The little ones clicked along the walls, running up the sides and the ceiling. The image pulled every childhood nightmare I could remember to the front.

But even that wasn't as terrifying as the disembodied black hand that held my ankle. It stuck out of the wall and began to pull me with it…*into* the wall!

"Sam! Mike!" I tried to grab anything I could to stop from being yanked hard into the wall I'd just bounced off of. But anything I grabbed broke and came away in my hands. Nothing happened. So whatever it was, the Grimoire didn't see it as a threat to…it.

"I can smell you!" Delilah's voice boomed down the tunnel.

The hand gave a hard, dislocating yank. I fell backward and landed in…

Water?

Damn *cold* water. I was disoriented and unable to figure out which way was out. My lungs screamed because I couldn't take in any more air. Something grabbed me around the shoulders and pulled me up.

When I broke free of the water I gasped and sputtered and kicked up a fuss.

"Calm down," Mike said gently in my ear. "I got you."

I held on to him as he pulled me out and then helped me sit on what felt like thick grass. A blue fire flickered, popped and crackled on the water's edge and after I'd gasped enough air I looked up from my prone position.

I saw stars.

Lots and lots of stars.

I saw the shadows of treetops, and the glowing eyes of owls as they looked down at me.

Something obscured the image and I looked into the black and shadowy face of… "What…the hell?" I managed to say, coughing all the way through.

"Hey, be nice, Dags. He just saved your ass," Sam moved into view and put a hand on the thing's shoulder. "Thank you."

You are welcome. It is not often I have visitors, and so I would cherish the time for talk. He refocused his featureless face on me. *I am Hob.*

I managed a weak smile. "Uh…hello Hob… I'm Dags."

He nodded and moved away. The best way I could describe the way he looked was a store mannequin, the kind with no features. Only this thing wasn't white, but black. Mike was still beside me and helped me sit up—and that's when the pain began. Fire ignited all along my right shoulder. I couldn't move my arm. I also lost hold of the present world and blacked out.

* * *

When I came to I was propped up against Mike, my entire right arm pinned to my chest with…silk?

He is awake.

Mike looked down and I returned his upside down gaze. "You look like shit. Are the shields still up?"

I nodded. I could still see the shimmer around him. "Yeah…what's wrong with my arm?"

"Same thing happened to Sam," he smiled. "Sort of missed a right tunnel and hit the wall. Only yours was more spectacular. Sam's arm's in a sling. You dislocated the whole thing and it looks like you cracked your collarbone. I'm afraid Sam can't heal you while she's under the protection spell. She's already tried. It's like we're encased in Teflon—except when we hit solid objects."

"Yeah," Sam said from where she sat on our left. "Too bad it doesn't work like armor to protect our physical bodies." Her right arm was in a sling of the same material. "But Hob said this," she said and nodded to the silk sling holding her arm in place. "This will heal us in a short time."

"What is this stuff?" I tried to sit up, and couldn't.

"You really don't wanna know—"

It is the spun silk of the Spiderwyk.

I blinked. "The what?"

It is the creature that works with me to guard the gate between the Cairn and Alfheim.

I frowned at Hob. "You're not talking about that huge drag queen spider that chased us?"

No. That is a Spriggan.

Of course. "Is *Alfheim* through that gate, past the Spiderwyk?"

Yes. It is only a small part of the world beyond the gate. He lifted an arm and gestured to an actual iron gate to the left, just across a small brook. The ironwork was detailed with gnarled trees and connected to a high wall of stone and trees.

"The fact the gate is made of iron…that's significant isn't it?"

Sam answered. "It is. It keeps the Fae from entering *Alfheim*. The Faeries don't want their creations to have access to their realm. Hob was telling us how the two queens, Medbh and Tzariene, while they don't agree on much, they do agree on segregation and discrimination."

Cheeky. "But the truth is the Faeries can't really travel past the Cairns, can they?"

No. Any time spent on this side causes the Faeries great pain, and prolonged time spent between the worlds has been known to grow madness.

"Interesting arrangement." I tried to sit up again and this time made it but not without Mike still supporting me. "Wish we had those kinds of safeguards set up between the Other Worlds and ours."

"We did," Sam said as she scooted closer. She pulled at a tall blade of grass and yanked it up. "But now there's just us. The Witches. Guarding the world's gates. It's like a game of whack-a-mole. You fix one hole and two more pop up. The Angels are the worst at setting rules and then breaking them."

The Angels have always wanted to rule the whole of existence. They began the war to spread their ideology and punished an entire realm for their transgressions against them. In the end, if they are not stopped, the universe will be swallowed up by them, and our realm, as well as the one you know as Abysmal, will disappear into the ethers of memory.

I asked, "So *Alfheim* isn't part of the known worlds?"

No.

"And it's not part of our world."

No.

I didn't really know how to interpret that.

Mike put a hand to my forehead. "We've been here too long. You've got a fever. We need to get out of here."

I smacked his hand away. "What about the dust?"

"Hob's agreed to give us some dust but he wants compensation. Not really for the dust itself, but for the damage your magic caused."

I swallowed as I looked at Hob. "I really did burn the Cairn, didn't I?"

Yes, and no. Medbh burned the bulk of the Cairn. Your escape enraged the queen so she punished us. But I know what Medbh's Changeling did to you and what she intended to do. Your power cannot fall into the hands of the queens, especially not even the mad queen.

I looked at Sam who said. "The mad queen—is that what you call Medbh?"

It is one of her names. But Medbh is just a discomfort inflicted on the realm. She rules Alfheim's *Obsidian Kingdom. There is a truly mad queen that rules this world. She is known as Charybdis.*

I stiffened. That sounded like a Revenant name. "Hob, is she a Faerie?"

I don't know. But I do not believe she and her brother were born here. Their lands are far from Alfheim *and they do not wander into the business of the Faerie.* He glided over the grass and knelt in front of us. *I would prefer a certain item from each of you. It will not cause you pain, nor will it hinder your release from the Cairn, which I can facilitate.*

I pushed myself up into a better position and Mike adjusted his own seat behind me.

From Samantha, I wish only a strand of hair.

She frowned, shrugged and tugged a strand of her dark hair out. With a quick nod she gave it to Hob.

He turned to me but I somehow knew he would speak to Mike first. *From you, a strand of hair also.*

Mike did the same thing Sam did and handed it to Hob.

I reached up to yank a strand of my own out, but Hob held up a hand. *From you, I wish a feather.*

All three of us sort of sat back a little. I narrowed my eyes. "A feather? I'm not sure if I have one."

But you have many. A single feather from you would allow me to begin the mending process of the Cairn. Medbh has abandoned it and will not return, but I cannot allow my home to wither away. It was not always a series of endless tunnels, Guardian. With it, I can rebuild it.

I held out my hand. "I understand and all, but, I don't have any feathers. I mean, you say I have many? Where?"

Hob tilted his head to his right shoulder and pointed at something behind me. *From your wings.*

GUARDiAN, AWAKE!

"What?"

The Fae glided up on his feet and held out his hands. *May I?*

I shrugged. "Sure?"

My back abruptly tingled. I sat up straight as a new weight pressed down on my shoulders. The weight wasn't exactly heavy—not *physically* heavy—but sort of astrally heavy. Not sure if that makes sense.

What I didn't expect was the look on Sam's face or how fast Mike scrambled away from me. What the hell was with them?

"That's just not possible...Hob, have those always been there?"

He was born a child of many worlds. The left hand of Hell, and the right hand of Heaven. His soul has been claimed by a very powerful book.

Right...left...what? I shifted and twisted around to see what they there were looking at—

Sprouting from my back, through my shirt, was a pair of half-folded wings. The right one opened as Hob stroked it. It was a white wing, with feathers the color of new snow. On the left flexed a black wing with feathers that reminded me of a raven's. I tried to get away from them, but they followed me and they moved and folded and braced against other objects.

"Dags...be careful or you'll wrench the other shoulder," Sam hobbled over on her knees. "Just remain calm and put your hand in mine."

I did as she said to do. Her hand was warm and soft.

I wish to have a feather of each. Is that possible?

"Yes...please...just make them go away." It wasn't that I didn't think it was cool; it was just frightening to me, to suddenly have wings.

Wings!

This would have been so much cooler in seventh grade. But right now?

"How come they're invisible?" Sam's tone pretty much mirrored the confusion I was feeling inside. "And how come we can see them now but not before?"

I felt a slight sting somewhere in my left shoulder, and then my right. The sensation was similar to pulling a hair from my head...only he was pulling a feather from my wings...that just...I put my unbound hand to my forehead. This was just, ridiculous.

Wings are a manifestation of the Guardian's duel nature. As I see it, it is an induced one, brought on by the concentration of essence in his chest. He manifested them some time ago, but he has not used them. His neglect has made them invisible and it has weakened them. I see the wings even when he does not. But I cannot see the physical makeup of the light burning within him. Hob stepped away with a black feather in his left hand, and a white one in his right. *Demonic as well as Angelic beings possess wings, though it is unclear why. They are not visible in your world because he does not believe they exist. But given the right control and power, they could, and he could fly.*

I didn't understand any of that. I reached behind me with my left hand, but the wings were gone.

"So he could actually make them appear and fly?"

Hob laughed, or he made a noise that sounded kinda like a laugh as he placed the feathers in a small basket with the strands of hair. *It would take a great deal of control. There are other creatures of a dual nature that can do this. I have heard of them but not seen them. Stories come to me here and I look into the waters sometimes.*

I thought of Gabriel, whose wingspan—when she presented them—rivaled the length of a 747.

Mike moved behind me and slipped a hand under my left shoulder to help me to my feet. "Hob, it was a pleasure meeting you. But I think we need to get out of here."

You fear the physical repercussions of returning to your world. Neither you nor the Witch will require this time as you are protected by magic, he turned to face me. *You are the one that will suffer. You've sacrificed in this Cairn already.*

"What does he mean you're going to suffer?" Sam narrowed her eyes at me. "What did you do?"

I ignored her and looked into Hob's non-face. "Hob, are you angry at me because Medbh burned the Cairn?"

He didn't answer at first and removed the silk sling from my shoulder and arm. I moved my arm around and closed my hand into a fist. No pain. *No. I was concerned, but you've given me the means to make repairs. And since Medbh's attention has now waned from this place, I do not fear her interference.*

"Could she though?" Sam asked as she stood and Hob approached her and removed her sling. "Could she mess up what you planned to do?"

Hob nodded.

"I suppose there's nothing we can do to stop her?"

When Hob didn't answer right away, I turned back to him.

The Fae abruptly turned into a puddle of dark, sparkling essence.

Faerie dust.

Take what you need. Behind you, Samantha, you will find bottles that will travel both worlds. But do not touch the dust itself.

Mike moved around me and helped Sam fill several of the bottles. They looked like glass with cork stoppers. Tear shaped. After they had three of them filled, using a few of the large leaves off a nearby tree as scoops, the dust shifted and became Hob again.

"So you're made of pure dust?"

Yes. All Cairns are created from creatures like me, and I carry the memories of those who were sacrificed. Don't concern yourself over touching me. I control the dust and you will not be influenced by it. Hob leaned his head forward. *I know what it is you hope to do, Guardian. And it is a dangerous gamble.*

I took a step back immediately and looked at Sam. "You told him?"

"It was the condition for him helping us."

Do not be angry, Guardian. I am not your enemy. Though you have many here in this Cairn alone. Most are not so forgiving for the damage that followed you.

Great.

You asked if there was something you could do, and freely giving me a part of each of you is enough. But if you leave this Cairn, it will be weeks before you are well enough to perform the magic you wish to create the facade, and months after you arrived.

"You mean Dags," Mike said. "But Sam and I could come back and meet with Medbh."

Yes. But without the Guardian's protection, when you returned would be in question, and the sickness would be upon you. Hob leaned his head to his left shoulder. *If you return at all.*

That sounded ominous. When I'd been in the Cairn before for what I believed was just a few hours, two weeks had passed in our world. I suspected we'd been in the Cairn for a lot longer this time, so if we left it'd be months later and we—I mean I—would lose even more time recovering. "Look, both of you. You're better off just doing this without me. I have the mantle and that's the only reason I'm here. Why I don't I just make the copy and you guys go ahead and get it done. I'll stay here with Hob and help him do whatever he's going to do with those…feathers. I know I'm mostly a liability—"

"Dags—" Sam said.

"No. Listen to me. I know I am. I can't fight worth a shit. I can't use a weapon—except for a sword I have no control over and no idea how to conjure, whatever the word is. You've had to heal me three times already, Sam. Come on. I'm just…" And there was where I faltered. "I'm not a hero. I wanted to be. I'm just some weird, screwed up guy with a book in his chest."

No one moved for a few seconds. I started to turn toward Hob to ask him how we could get Mike and Sam to Medbh. I didn't expect Mike to move at the same time. And I sure as hell didn't expect him to knock me on my ass with a right cross. The pain stung my nose and I tasted blood in the back of my throat as I landed.

"Mike! What are you doing?" Sam's voice echoed off the stone walls of Hob's grotto.

I wiped my nose with the back of my hand. It came away with blood on it.

"Who the hell *are* you?" Mike yelled as he looked down at me. "You're not the Darren McConnell I remember. That Dags was cocky and fearless. He wasn't afraid of anything, or if he was, he never let me see it. The Darren I remember helped me through a divorce, taught me how the world really works, and told me the only way around any problem was to go through it." He put his hands on his hips. "When I met you, I thought you were some spoiled pretty-boy. White bread educated know-it-all. Looked up your dad and saw he had money. And I knew I was right." He shook his head. "I was wrong. You had more confidence in your right pinky finger than I ever had my whole entire life. You showed me the world wasn't as fucked up as I believed it was. I depended on you more than you'll ever know, more than you realize. I don't know what all happened to you in the past two years… but it killed you. It destroyed the best friend I thought I had. It beat you down."

Best friend? I stared up at him, bleeding from my nose. The backs of my eyes burned when I saw his face. The look of shame, disappointment and ill-conceived frustration. He wasn't kidding. Mike was really, really upset with me.

He called me his best friend.

The only sound was the trickle of water from the waterfall into the pond and sound of distant thunder from the rolling clouds beyond the gate. I wiped my nose on my sleeve and pushed myself up on my feet. I knew I looked bad. A nosebleed, ripped shirt, and I was pretty sure I had a nasty look on my face. It was one thing to suspect my best friend was disappointed. It was a whole other thing to hear him say it.

"Mike—" Sam's voice was small. But Mike just waved her away and turned his back on me.

"Let's go. Thomas was right. Bringing him was a bad idea. We'll do better to infiltrate this queen's palace and find her ourselves without this mantle."

"Mike—" I said, trying to rein in my boiling temper. "You can't do that. You'll just get yourself caught. You need the mantle to trade for her. I know you—"

"What the hell do you know?" He turned at that moment and I saw his fighting face. The one I used to see when he'd get into fights after Teresa wanted the divorce and threatened to take Brendi from him. Was it possible he wanted to pick a fight with me? "You vanished off the face of the planet when I needed you, when my world fell in on itself and I was arrested because they thought I killed Teresa. They still think I killed Brendi! And now you show up with this power and you can't even use it!"

I balled my hands into fists. "I don't know how to use it!"

"Really? You caught yourself on fire. You caught a whole Cairn on fire. You snuffed out an army of possessed plants—and you don't know how to use it?" He snarled at me. "Bullshit! You're afraid of using it. You're just a small, meek little mama's boy." Mike straightened. "Oh wait…you can't even remember your mama cause you were born in a tree!"

That pissed me off. I wasn't the kind of person to verbally assault and then just walk off. I needed closure. I was also feeling very, very stung, which just fueled that anger. Mike moved to his pack and bent down over it.

Something stirred inside of my chest, somewhere around a tight, raw bundle of nerves had grown comfortable. I pulled my hands into fists as his words rolled around in my head, mimicking the thunder. My shock twisted and then unraveled that bundle until it coiled neatly where it should be. I saw the book in front of me, the pages flipping furiously. When they stopped I saw the connection, the spell, the missing piece.

A piece I didn't realize I needed until then.

I held out my hands. *"Ati me peta babka!"*

The book exploded as pages flew out and moved single-file around the room. Whether the others could see it, I didn't care. I could. I watched as they split in two and entered my outstretched palms. The impact was both subtle and overwhelming. The bundle coiled inside of me strengthened and connected to my core. Everything connected to me.

As the procession of pages came to an end, those wings came out again. I couldn't spread them as far as I wanted because the grotto wasn't big enough. But I could feel them. I knew they were there now. It was like those days sitting in front of a computer and needing to get up and stretch my legs.

I could see the book in its entirety. Even pages that had no business being there. I would weed those out soon as I rearranged them the way I wanted them. I found the sword and called it to me as my anger spun forward and concentrated on the back of the one that hurt me.

The one friend I still believed in.

But as I lunged, intent on striking him from behind, he turned and blocked my sword with his long knife. Our eyes met and he was… smiling.

My anger, my hurt, and even my ego paused when I saw that smile. Then he laughed.

"Now *that*, is the Darren McConnell I remember," he said over our crossed weapons.

I blinked a few times and stood back, folding my wings but I kept my sword raised. He lowered his own and stood there grinning at me. That's when I remembered why the words hurt so much. Why they rang so harsh inside of me. "I told you the same thing when Teresa filed the divorce papers. I called you a coward, a peacemaker. I…told you to get out there and fight for your daughter."

"Yeah. You did. I was ready to give it all up. We were in my store and you brought over a six-pack of some cheap beer. You started that shit with me and you came this close," he held up his hand and indicated a very small space between his index finger and thumb. “To getting your ass kicked that night. But you were right. I got my butt in gear and I fought back. Teresa was impressed and I got full custody. The store started making money. And I finally felt like I was in control again.”

The sword vanished, and the wings as well, as I shook my head. Mike looked to be okay with what just happened, but I wasn't. “I really hate you some times.”

Mike winked. “I know.” He held out his hand.

I stared at it, but didn't take it. “I'm gonna need a little more time.”

He gave a short sigh and lowered his hand. “Awright.”

Sam moved to stand between us. She looked to Mike, then me, then Mike again. “What the hell just happened?”

Hob clapped his hands. *A wonderful thing, Samantha! The Guardian is now awake!*

THE PLAN

Sam threw up her hands and moved away. "Men…" she muttered.

Mike tossed his long knife aside and we did the bro-hug. Clasp the opposite hand, hug and slap each other's back. But it felt different. It felt…close. Mike was my best friend. But there was something more. He was like a brother to me.

I turned to Hob and realized…I felt great! I put my hand to my nose and it didn't hurt. "Did I just heal my nose?"

The Grimoire did. Sam asked what happened. You and the book are connected now. You are truly one.

I looked at Hob and then at Sam and Mike. "Is that a good thing?"

Sam shrugged. "I'm guessing he means a connection has formed between the book and those portals in your hands. Your magic should be working. Although, I wouldn't suggest trying fire. Not in a closed space."

"Oh. Uh uh. No experimenting. Not now. We have to make a plan."

Mike nodded and looked at Hob. "I think I can speak for all three of us when I say, we're doing it *now*. No leaving until I have my daughter. Can you help us?"

Yes. For a price.

Damn Faeries and their deals.

"What's the catch?"

Hob paused. *Conversation.*

"You want us to give you conversation in return for your help?"

Yes.

"Deal," Sam said before anyone could jump in. I followed up, and then Mike.

Hob gestured for us to come close to him. When we did, he led us to the water's edge and pointed at the still surface. *Queen Medbh celebrates the Wild Hunt with a dance near her home in the Obsidian lands. Not the Obsidian castle. It is at this time she will be most vulnerable because she will be surrounded by her admirers. She will also be most powerful because she is at her power base.*

The water shifted and an image of a grand home of spires and sharp crystal angles appeared. That was Medbh's home? The image pulled back to show a rolling landscape of dark clouds to the right over what looked like ruins. To the left, the sun shown bright with white rays reflecting off of what looked like a glass lake and crystal trees. This looked like someone's nightmare.

"When you say the Wild Hunt, you mean the legendary Hunt across the worlds where the Faeries search for humans with their hounds?" Sam got down on her hands and knees to look at the pictures.

Yes. During certain times the veil between the worlds is thinnest and the Faeries Hunt. The queen spreads before them a carpet of Faerie mist so they cannot touch the ground. My opinion is you will have the perfect opportunity to present Medbh with the substitute mantle at that time. And in order to appear thankful, she will grant whatever wish you have. But the potency of the mantle will only last a few hours, measurements of time that only have meaning in your world.

"So you're saying it could fall apart right after we make it, or years down the road."

Precisely. Once she grants your wish you have to get back here as soon as you can. You have to come here and no other Cairn. Your time with her will give me the space I need to repair the Cairn and make a new gate. But to her it will appear as broken as she left it. Even she will not step through.

I heard something in his voice and looked over at Hob. "You mean *she* won't, but that doesn't mean she won't send Fae."

Hob nodded. *But you should be safely back in your world by then.*

Sam sat back. "Hob—we can't stay here that long. And you're talking about going physically into *Alfheim.* That's not a good idea. A Cairn is bad enough, but *into* the land of Faerie itself?"

I leaned to my right to try and catch some kind of hint in Hob's blank face as to what he wasn't telling us. "That's what you want the conversation for. You know how to cross without sickness or the movement of time?"

With the items you gave me, I can weave your essence into the Cairn's matrix. That will allow you to go back and forth without physical duress. But as for the time...I do not control it. And it's not predictable. You could step out a second after you entered, or a century. That is a risk you will have to take.

Mike said, "I'm willing to do anything to get my daughter back."

Hob looked at me. *Release the spell and replenish your strength.*

I did as he asked, imagining clipping the ties to Mike and Sam. The sparkling around them vanished and I felt better instantly. It felt like a weight was gone. Literally.

"Hob," Sam toyed with the crystal hanging from her earring. "I'm assuming we can walk in *Alfheim* as humans? Our presence won't sound an alarm?"

Faeries take very little notice of humans who wander into Alfheim *even during the Hunt. Unless the intrusion happens on their lands, then the intruder is usually used as sport. I will cast a glamour on you so the guards won't detain you, but once you enter her home, my glamour will fade. Getting in to see Medbh will be simple since she believes no one would dare harm her. Whatever happens, do not let her guards take you to her dungeons. If you are held there, I cannot rescue you and those kept there are often forgotten, both in* Alfheim *and in the Physical World.*

"Great," Sam stood up. "What about Dags? Won't his unique abilities sort of show up on the magic-dar?"

Hob looked at me. *While in the Cairn, Medbh's Changeling toyed with you. It suspected there was something different about you. But it was like looking through a filter. If the Changeling had brought you into* Alfheim *itself, there would be a disturbance. A whisper of something. But I do not think they will see it, unless you use your magic. If you do, every creature in this world will know you're here and they'll be drawn to you like—*

I held up my hand. "Yeah, yeah, moths and flame and shit. No magic."

Correct. Do not take my warning lightly, Guardian. They will try and take you. Keep you. Bind you to them. Use you. Protect yourself and protect your friends because they are one of your greatest weaknesses.

"So…I'd be going in there with no access to magic or any means to protect us?"

It is the only way to hide what you are. Samantha would still be able to use her magic. They do not view human magic as a threat against their own Arcane.

Sam blinked. "Well they're right. My magic can't fight Arcane. That stuff's…dangerous."

Your guns can do damage. I suggest using them.

Sam reached out and patted Mike's shoulder. "Looks like you're on point."

Mike pulled his bag to him and removed two handguns. He checked the ammo in their barrels before he handed both of them to Sam, grip first. "These are 625 JM Smith & Wessons."

Sam took them, one in each hand. The smile on her face looked almost orgasmic. "Sweet Lady. Forty-five caliber, six rounds. Oh I'm well aware of these beauties."

"Good," Mike smiled. "I thought you said you could fire handguns."

"Oh yes I can. Faster and quicker than spells." Sam tucked them into the back of her jeans.

I have one more warning. Do not eat anything while in Alfheim. *The food is created with the essence contained in the dust. Do not even drink water. Be aware not only of the temptation of food, but of the lure of the dust. One touch of that dust against your skin and you will be forever owned by whatever creature held it.*

Got it. Don't eat, pray a lot, and love the idea of going home.

"Do we have a guarantee Medbh going to uphold her promise of a wish?" Mike crossed his arms.

She will have to. The Faeries are very serious about their oaths, and if she believes she has that mantle then you three will become less important, he looked at me. *But this will only be true as long as she cannot see your power. In order for you to get away from her, you must return here. I cannot help you if you do not return to* this *Cairn into my grotto. If you try and return through the main entrance, you will suffer.*

"And you'll get us back home with no problems?" Sam leaned her head toward Hob.

I will do my best.

"Why?" Everyone turned to look at me. I shrugged. "Sorry but why? Every weird ass creature I've met has either tried to take my power, eat me or kill me. Why are you helping?"

Hob hung his head. *I am...lonely.*

That...wasn't the answer I was expecting and I felt like shit for being such an ass. "Lonely?"

I live as part of this pool. As part of all the pools before the Cairns. I see what comes and what goes. They do not acknowledge me; they simply believe I am there to serve them. I have been lonely for so very long, with no one to talk to. When I saw the Cairn destroyed, I believed this existence would come to an end and I would find peace. But then I heard your footsteps and saw in the pool the Spriggan chasing you through the remnants of the Cairn. I took a chance and made myself known to the Witch. Hob turned and looked at Sam who smiled at him. *And she did not run in terror. She came to me and spoke to me, she thanked me and hugged me...when we pulled you to safety.* He looked back at me. *I am an Urisk and I crave companionship. I see life go by, but I cannot touch it. And you...* he turned to all of us. *You saw me as something more.*

If I wasn't careful, I was going to get teary eyed. To my surprise, Sam opened up her arms and gave Hob another hug. His black form shimmered and I thought I saw features in that blank, black face. Or maybe it was my imagination.

Hob pulled away. He looked embarrassed. *I want to help you so that you will come back now and then? And talk to me?*

Mike and I glanced at one another. I stuck out my hand to Hob. "How can we refuse?"

ALFHEiM

We had a plan and the stupidity to see it through.

Now all we needed was to make the mantle. Hob prepared an area for us. And by prepared, I mean he moved away grass, dirt and flowers until only stone remained. Sam built a fire in the center of the clearing, and then used one of the partially burnt pieces of wood to draw a pentagram around the fire. I sat to the side, trying to figure out how I was going to do this. Thomas put the mantle into the book, so how did I use it to make a facade?

I wasn't going to be able to use the book in *Alfheim*, so I figured I'd better make good use of it now. While Sam worked, I closed my eyes and asked the book how to make the mantle. Seemed simple enough. And as always the book appeared, the pages flipped, until they landed on the new page, the one Thomas had slipped in.

That's when things got real. Up until then I just had the intent, put some feeling behind it and spoke the language of the Grimoire, or at least the earlier parts of the Grimoire. There were a lot of languages in this book. But this time I moved without thinking. I knew on some level the Grimoire was in charge, or at least I suspected it was. I reached out to Sam and asked for a vial of the dust.

She handed one to me. I poured it onto the stone in front of me in the form of a rectangle. Then filled it in until the bottle was empty. I felt Sam's and Mike's eyes on me as I held my hand over the rectangle and felt something weave and tumble down my arm. A glance at it and I wished I hadn't looked.

Tiny white spiders oozed out of my skin and crawled to my hand. They jumped onto the rectangle and began spinning webs. Red silk. Hundreds of them came. There were so many of them they fell over each other. My body was locked where it was, a conduit for the book of total annihilation.

The rectangle glowed red, sparkled and then the spiders vanished. The book let go and I was on my feet, shaking the ick off of me like a girl who just found a bug down her bra. After I finished my little fit, I looked at the stone.

In place of the dust lay a perfectly folded red mantle. Or a facade of it. With a glance at Sam and Mike, I tentatively touched it. The fabric was as soft as silk. Spider silk. I held it between both hands. "It feels real."

It is real. The dust is what will convince Medbh it is the veil she seeks.

I refolded it and handed it off to Mike. "You keep it. You need to be the one to ask for the exchange."

He took it as if it were made of glass and carefully tucked it into his back pocket. "It's not going to disappear before we can use it, right?"

It should not. But there is always a chance. If the facade does vanish, I would suggest building another one quickly.

No shit. I would have suggested going ahead and making another one. But my muscles ached when I moved them. My shoulders and lower back hurt and I was pretty sure if I laid down, I'd fall asleep. And I did not want to sleep in a Cairn. There were just too many things in the place that set off my danger meter.

"So would this wish she offered be different than the actual exchange between the mantle and Brendi?" Sam asked. "Why not just use the wish to ask for Brendi back?"

Hob held out his hand. *If she were honorable, that would be enough. But Medbh is cunning and like all of her kind, will try to cheat you out of a deal. She can only do this with one deal, not two. If she manages to trick you out of the trade, she cannot denounce the wish.*

Sam brushed the pentagram away with her boot just before she carried water from the stream in one of the glass bottles and doused the fire. "I think we need to get going."

Yes. Once you pass through the gate you have to cross over the wastes to get to Alfheim.

"Wastes?" Sam and I said together.

She took over. "You didn't mention wastes before. What are the wastes?"

Hob held out his hand and a small, flat disk formed out of whatever he was made of. *This is a compass, but it only works in* Alfheim. *It will point you to the queen's home.* He handed it to me. It looked just like any ordinary compass...except for the runes on the face. At the moment the needle didn't move no matter which way I turned it.

"Hob...don't avoid my question. What are the wastes?" Sam tapped her foot.

I slipped the compass into my back pocket and glanced over my shoulder, half expecting to see a wing back there. I was relieved I didn't.

The wastes are what is left of the warlands.

"Warlands?" Mike had pulled out his huge gun and checked his magazines again. "You mean there was a war in Faerie?"

We were invaded a long time ago by another world. Our leaders destroyed their...heroes, Hob turned to Sam. *They did not win, but neither did the Faerie. The warlands are where the battles raged. One of their sons set this world on fire.*

"Are the wastes dangerous?" I asked.

Yes. They're filled with creatures that would love the chance to take you, use you and ride your dead shell back to your world. So I would advise caution.

I started to say something but Sam put a hand on my shoulder. "Is there any way to avoid the wastes?"

Hob put a finger to his chin. *There is a way—but I do not know if it still works.*

"What is it?" she kept her hand on my shoulder.

The Faeries create a pathway—a line—that gives them a corresponding end. If you were to find that correspondence point, and if Medbh did not destroy it, then it is possible to avoid the wastes. But if you take the wrong line, another Faerie's perhaps, then I don't know where you would end up.

Mike chuffed. "You mean teleport. Medbh set up a teleporting thing."

"Sounds like a ley line," Sam looked at Hob.

Yes. They are ley lines. I can show you where it might be.

Sam pulled her hand back. "We'll risk it. Uh…is the way we're dressed fine?"

Yes. Hob glided across the grass to the stream where he walked on top of the water to the opposite shore and gate. Myself, Sam and Mike went through the water but weren't even wet when we stepped out on the opposite side.

Hob touched the lock on the gate and instantly the chains fell aside. The gate doors creaked open, swinging away from us toward what looked like a park in autumn. There was even a bench in front of an oak. I looked around at the cave Hob lived in and noticed it wasn't so much the Cairn encroaching on the world of *Alfheim*, but the opposite. Faerie had spilled through the gate like ivy running under the neighbor's fence.

The ley line Medbh used will be marked. Since I cannot leave the Cairn, I do not know what the mark is. But you will know it when you see it.

Sam reached out and hugged Hob again before she stepped through the gate. Mike shook his hand and gave him a pat on the back. When he and I faced each other, his face shifted both shape and color. With his back to the others, they didn't see Hob look at me with the face of Thomas. *Heed what I said, Guardian, about the wish. The future's not written in stone and it does not depend on your past.*

I was a bit confused about his and Thomas's advice on the wish, especially since we might have to use it to get Brendi back if the exchange falls apart. Hob reached out and embraced me then, and I inhaled a spicy, musky scent I hadn't noticed before. When he stepped back, Hob's face was back to the black, blank facade of a department store mannequin. I gathered my wits—which of course had tried to abandon me in a moment of OMG!—and walked through the gate to join Mike and Sam.

The lush jungle we stepped into didn't last long. Within a ten-minute walk, the high grass and thick, gnarled trees disappeared and were replaced by…nothing. The landscape shifted into barren, cracked dirt. Miles and miles of it. Even the color of the world changed from lush greens, blues and whites to burnt orange, brown and black. In the distance we could see a cityscape that looked like any other cityscape. The sky behind it looked ominous. I hoped like hell that wasn't where we were supposed to go, so when I took the compass out of my pocket, my heart fell into my feet when the arrow pointed in front of us.

"That's Faerie Land?" Sam pointed to the looming city. "Looks more like…*Escape from New York* or something."

"According to this, that's *Alfheim*," I said. "But I'm beginning to think none of this is really Faerie like we learned about as a kid."

"Uh uh," Mike shook his head. "So…I'm assuming that area between here and there is the wastes?"

I think we all agreed on that assumption. So we drew our weapons, except for me. Because if I used my weapon I'd wake up bad things. "Hob said Medbh's line would be marked. Do any of you see an obvious mark?"

We dispersed along the border, keeping on the grass and looking desperately for something—

"I found it!"

Mike and I hurried over to Sam who stood directly in front of the path back to the Cairn. She pointed up. Floating about a foot or two above us was a large sign that read, *Quack like a duck.*

"That can't be serious."

I looked at Sam and quacked.

And found myself at the gate of the distant city.

What the—

A small pop of air and Mike appeared. Then Sam.

"Did anyone else just have a fast forward moment?" Mike looked around us while I stared up at the huge double doors to the city. I couldn't see the tall buildings and spires we'd seen in the distance. The only view we had was of a massive wall. Why would anyone need a wall that big?

"Yeah...and I'm not sure it's making me comfortable." Sam held her pistol with the barrel down. "There's a smaller door to the right of the larger one. Try that one."

"You want me to ring the bell?" Mike approached the door but he didn't sound all that confident.

"I don't see a bell," I said as I came up behind him.

Mike tried the knob and it turned. With a glance back at us he pushed it in. Nothing spectacular happened. No explosion or attack of killer bees. We simply stepped through another door into a thick, humid garden. Butterflies in colors I've never seen on butterflies came to greet us as we stepped in.

The door closed behind us with a heavy thud. When we turned to look—no door.

"That's worrisome," I said.

"I've got a bad feeling about this." Mike moved in front of Sam and I and brushed the butterflies off.

That's when they started biting. Little pretties had big teeth! We batted at them, keeping them away from our faces and took off through the garden. It wasn't at all like Hob's garden...in fact...it looked a lot like Mike's garden behind his townhouse. When I tried to avoid going further into the garden, the butterflies came at me with teeth. They did the same with Mike and Sam. As long as we stayed on a path leading into the garden's center—they flew along side us and didn't bite.

We heard the murmuring of voices before we saw anyone. The soft hum of chamber music. The focal point of the garden was a large shallow marble pool filled with water. In the center sat an empty pedestal. As we passed through a rose trimmed archway, the garden abruptly filled with people of all sizes and shapes. Or they looked like people. Actually...they looked like people would in the court of King Louis XIV. Lots of gold trim on waistcoats, collars and sleeves, large poofy skirts, powdered white wigs and loads of makeup. As the butterflies herded us closer to the pond, I saw lilies in a wicked pallet of colors floating in the water and I could make out multi-colored koi as well.

"Ah…the entertainment is here!" a woman's voice rang clear over the murmuring.

We turned to see a rather short woman dressed in red silks descend a marble staircase from a marble balcony. The guests parted quickly to allow her to pass through to us. I stood by the pond, with Mike to my right and Sam to my left. Was this…Medbh?

"Welcome, welcome…" she gushed as she curtsied in front of us. "I am Queen Medbh, ruler of the Obsidian Court. Oh…the Spriggan sent me a variety this time! How wonderful! A tall handsome human, and a Witch!" Her eyes cut to me and narrowed. "I'm afraid I'm not sure what you are. But you do smell…familiar."

Medbh couldn't have been over sixteen years old. On the outside. I wasn't stupid enough to think this is what she *really* looked like. If there was one thing I was getting used to, it was not trusting what I saw. Though she moved and squealed like an adolescent girl, I felt her power.

"My Queen," a tall man in a black and gold costume stepped closer. "Are you sure these are the ones Delilah told you about?"

Delilah? Our Delilah?

We all glanced at each other. Crap. The drag queen spider thing had ratted us out!

"Well of course they are. Just as it described, though this one," she said and reached out between Sam and Mike to grab for me. "*Is* a bit different."

Sam brought the barrel of one of her guns up and pressed it into the elbow of Medbh. I know what it's like to bang my elbow, so when Medbh jerked her arm back I was pretty sure it hurt. Or it could have been the iron in the metal of the gun. The look on Medbh's face said she was about to do really bad things to Sam.

"Your Highness," I said and stepped forward to make sure she didn't keep Sam on her radar. "I'm not sure what Delilah told you about us, but we wanted an audience with you because we found something we learned belongs to you."

Her attention snapped from Sam to me and her frown righted itself in record speed. "Oh? You have something of mine? How can I be sure you didn't steal it?"

"I give you my word." Yeah, it sounded lame but I accented it with a really deep bow. We needed to get Brendi and get the hell out of there now.

"Well…that's got to be the most respect any human thing has ever shown me. Better than the rot that showed up here today." She glanced around, indicating her guests. "So," she said and clasped her hands in front of her. "What is it you're sure you didn't take?"

I stepped in front of Sam just to make sure she stayed invisible as Mike came forward.

Medbh's smile widened as she looked up at him. "Did you steal it?"

"No Queen Medbh." He went down on one knee so he was eye-level with her. When he pulled the mantle from his back pocket, a hush fell over the crowd. Everyone hovered over us, looking down at the delicate fabric in his hand. I just hoped the thing didn't pick that moment to vanish.

Medbh's expression wasn't anywhere close to readable. Her eyes focused on the mantle for several seconds before she looked into Mike's face. "Where…did you get this?"

"From a man in my world. He said he took it from you to protect my world. I wish to trade this for the return of my daughter."

Her eyes narrowed on Mike's face. "Your daughter?"

"Brendi Ross. Your Changeling took her and murdered her mother. I would like to trade this for her."

A murmur rose in the crowd as everyone gathered close to watch. I felt the electricity of excitement tinge the air.

Medbh plastered the smile back on her face. "My dear boy, you've braved a great deal to return this to me. But how do I tell you were not the one to take it?"

"I am a mortal in his mid thirties, Queen Medbh," he took in a deep breath. "The man I took it from said he received this centuries ago."

"I see."

One sullen looking woman with a large mole over her lip waved a fan in her face. "I can see we're not going to have any entertainment tonight."

Medbh shot her a narrowed glance and the fan turned into a bird that pecked at the woman's face. The woman backed up, screaming as blood and bits of skin flew out in all directions. She turned and ran blindly into a nearby wall. The bird settled on her back to finish the job. The others watched the display, sighed and then returned their attention to us.

What the hell kind of place is this?

I felt Sam's fingers against mine and I glanced back at her. She felt the same apprehension. And the same fear that things were going to go south, regardless of Thomas's assurances. I was busy thinking up ways to get out of there. I looked back the way we came and knew we just had to run back down the path past the rose-covered arch.

"You are right, dear boy. You are but a man, and the Witch with you with the defiant hand is even younger. But this…one…" She reached out to take the mantle but Mike pulled it away.

"My daughter, Queen Medbh. And then we shall trouble you no more."

"Indeed." She pursed her lips. Her brows arched. "Your daughter is a God Mother's bastard."

"She has the God Mother's blood, Queen Medbh."

Medbh narrowed her eyes until they were slits. The sky overhead darkened just a bit. Not like a big dramatic show but it was noticeable. And not just by me. "I now realize who your companion is, mortal. And why he angers me," she smiled, and I didn't like the look of it. "Are you quite sure the only thing you wish to trade for is your daughter?"

Before Mike could answer, I felt Sam's hand jerk away from me. The crowd made an "awwww" sound as I turned to see why she pulled back. But what I saw nearly drove me to my knees.

Sam wasn't with me anymore. In fact…Sam wasn't even human. A statue now stood on the pedestal, a perfectly carved replica of Samantha. Her face looked up at the sky as water poured from the barrel of her pistol.

"Sam!" Mike yelled out as he pulled the mantle away and stood next to me. I risked a second to touch her.

But she wasn't flesh anymore. And this wasn't a replica. Samantha had been transformed into cold marble.

THE OATH

"You bitch!" Mike pulled his gun in a flash and aimed it at Queen Medbh, the barrel centimeters from her nose. "You make her right."

"Is that your trade, mortal? You want the life of your girlfriend for returning to me what is rightfully mine?" She straightened her back as she crossed her arms over her chest and grew in size until she was three feet taller than anyone else, guests included. "Is that your trade?"

Mike glanced over at Sam. "You never intended to keep a promise, did you? You are indeed the Mad Queen. A liar and a thief."

"Me? A thief?"

"You stole what wasn't yours, Medbh. My daughter was never yours to take. Just like this mantle was never yours."

Medbh leaned forward. "She was a Witch. And I *claim* Witches," she pointed at Sam. "I claim her! And that mantle is mine!"

"You can't have her. Where is my daughter?"

"Is that your trade? To see where she is and not have her back?" Medbh's gaze flickered over to the Sam statue. "Or do you want to rescue your friend before the transformation is final and she dies?"

"How do I know they're both alive?" Mike removed the safety. "You give me Brendi or I will put a hole through your skull."

Then Medbh's gaze slid to me. "Really, mortal? You'll shoot me?"

I knew something was coming before she did it. I just didn't know what. Hob had said not to use the book, but how in the hell else were we going to get out of this? It was pretty damn obvious Medbh was going to find any loophole to crawl through and the guests looked as if they were just there for the entertainment. When she pointed at me I ducked and rolled into the crowd. Whatever she fired hit the edge of the fountain and a few of the guests who didn't move fast enough. They immediately turned to stone.

Shit!

"Queen Medbh! What are you doing?" her guests called out. "It is a fair trade!"

"Do not think to judge me! I do what I want!" Medbh screamed as she pointed at me again, and again I ducked away from her—just not fast enough. Something struck my shoe and my foot and ankle went numb. It gave under me and I landed behind a woman with an incredibly huge skirt.

I heard Mike's gun go off and then a hush. Mike knelt over me. "You okay?"

"I can't feel..." I had to re-evaluate. "I can't feel my leg."

"That's because it's stone," he said as he tried to help me up.

The woman whose skirt I hid behind grabbed Mike's shoulder. He started to bring the gun up to fire at her but she pushed it down, grabbed his wrist and pulled him down beside me. Her gaze locked with mine. "You...you can't be here. I made sure you couldn't ever be here!"

I stared into her beautiful face. It was oval shaped, with light gray eyes, dark lashes and ruby red lips. Pearls were woven through dark tresses that hung around her shoulders. She had the palest skin. Her delicate ears, visible between the curls, tapered off into delicate points. I opened my mouth to ask if I knew her, but the pain of the transformation took my breath. I looked at my foot—the stone had moved from my foot and ankle and was rapidly moving over my knee.

"Lady," Mike said in a harsh, low voice as the guests screamed and ran around us. "If you don't let go of him—"

The woman continued gripping Mike's wrist. "You have to get him out of here. This is the one place he cannot stay! Have either of you eaten anything?"

Mike's expression shifted from anger to slight confusion. "No—"

"Drank anything?"

"No. We just got here."

"Have you touched dust?"

"No! Lady—"

"Then the queen's magic won't last. Hob was right to send you here still cloaked in the magic of your world. Your friend will revert back to herself in a few seconds, just as Darren's leg will reverse itself within the next few seconds. Both of them will be weak but you've all got to leave!"

I stared at her face. She knew my name? Not my nickname, but my real name. She sounded and looked so…*familiar.* I noticed the fur on her dress. At her neckline and then at her wrists. Wolf fur. "Do… do you know Brendi?" I asked because that seemed the logical way she knew my name. I could hear the shush of pages turning. The Grimoire wasn't happy. I could *feel* it.

The lady looked back at me when she released Mike's wrist and put her hand on my face. Her skin was cold. Ice cold. "Yes. Please…you must forget Brendi. Forget this place. It will only bring you heartache."

A pendant at her neck moved in the subdued light. A silver disk with a red stone, a moon and a wolf. I recognized the image—but—that wasn't possible!

Guests continued screaming and running, but I didn't hear Medbh's voice.

I'd started shaking as the cold of the marble moved up my thigh, but at a much slower pace. I couldn't take my eyes off her face as images flashed back to me. And the words, *I love you.* "M-mom?"

I sensed as well as saw Mike's reaction. He looked from me, to this lady, and back to me. "What?"

She smiled at me. "You have to go."

"Not without my daughter!" Mike hissed.

She tore her gaze from me and something subtle changed in her face. "You have to forget your daughter, Mike Ross. She isn't the same child you remember. Nothing can change that. She is alive. She is thriving here. But if you don't get my son out of *Alfheim,* I will personally destroy her myself." As she spoke those subtle shifts in her face became less subtle and more…terrifying.

Mike brought his gun up and pressed it to her head. "Where is my daughter?"

No! I gritted my teeth against the numbing pain and grabbed his gun. He wasn't prepared for that. It went off. Luckily, the bullet went wild.

A word, a spell, nearly tumbled from my lips. Something to stop him from doing something stupid. But I wasn't as fast as my mom's fist. She landed a jaw cracking left cross that snapped his head to his left. "Don't be a fool," she hissed at him. "Medbh's *not* dead."

"Did you shoot her?" I asked.

Mike put his hand to jaw and worked it back and forth. "Right between the eyes. It won't keep her down but it'll keep her—"

A scream pierced the conversation and guests scattered with an increased speed to the farthest ends of the garden. Queen Medbh, with a bleeding bullet hole through her forehead, stood in the center of the now empty space. Blood black as tar streamed to either side of her nose like war paint. Her skin bleached white and her hair turned black. And oh god she was getting taller.

I turned to my mom—but she was gone. I looked around to see if I could see her in the crowd, but there was nothing. Just faces of terrified guests in their period costumes. A familiar tingling started behind at my back, between my shoulder blades. I held onto Mike as he slipped an arm behind my back and pulled me to my feet. My good knee buckled and Mike had to fully support my weight as well as hold his gun steady on Medbh.

"Dags…I'm losing you."

And he was. I lost all feeling from the waist down and now it was working up over my stomach and my lungs—the stone spell was traveling up from my foot and spreading to the rest of my body. It wasn't slowing anymore.

Medbh laughed. "Damn Daoine Sidhe! Thought she could still my magic!"

I gasped at the pressure on my chest. I couldn't breathe and tried to hold onto Mike. He looked from me to Medbh and back, and finally leaned over enough for me to roll onto the ground, gasping like a fish out of water.

"Are you sure your trade is for your daughter?" she mocked him and laughed as she took a rumbling step closer. "Maybe you should choose between saving your friends?"

"Make a wish for the mantle," said a crow as it landed on the top of a woman's tall wig. "Fair trade, make a wish!"

"Shut up, Puck!" She pointed at the bird and something black shot from her finger. The crow avoided the hit and disappeared.

All the guests were nodding in agreement.

Mike leveled the gun at Medbh again. "I know that bullet hurts. And I've got plenty more. Now, you can hand over my daughter and return my friends to normal, or I can start shooting you and your guests."

What guests remained yelled and started running about.

Medbh laughed. "Give me my mantle or I'll kill them both!"

The crow returned. "Liar! Liar! Medbh's on fire!" Puck called out again and took off.

Mike aimed at her face. "He's right. You're a liar and you'll never have this mantle."

"Enough!" She charged at Mike, but something struck her from the left side and knocked her several feet into a line of guests. Mike and I both looked over to see the upper part of Sam's body moving from the fountain, but she was still stone from there down. Apparently she'd fired off some kind of magic whammy at the raving bitch of a queen.

"Sam!" Mike started toward her.

"Dags!" she screamed. "Use the damned book!"

I wanted to call out and remind her that Hob said not to—but I doubt Hob thought this was going to happen. And I knew she was thinking the same thing. It was a bitch to concentrate on the book when I couldn't breathe. But it didn't seem to matter as the images came fast and I was knocked out of the driver's seat once again.

The stone spell began vanishing for me the same as it was for Sam. Air rushed into my lungs as I bounced onto my still numb feet. A flaming black sword sprang from my left hand and I grabbed it in both as I took a ready stance facing Queen Medbh as she got back to her feet.

"You!" Recognition raged behind her eyes and she produced a sword to match my own. "I know you now. You destroyed my Cairn."

"*You* destroyed your Cairn, you dumbass," I heard myself say. Not exactly Peter Parker level banter, but it was the best I could do while the book directed my movements. I actually forced an attack with a hacking slash. Medbh defended with a strong parry and then tried to undercut with a turn. But whomever was driving my body knew what they were doing and managed to twist in a way I couldn't have as I jumped over the swinging blade and brought my blade down and sideways against her exposed neck.

The blade actually struck home but didn't go cleanly through. Not enough momentum and thrust, and I was at an odd angle. I didn't actually know all this, but the driver did.

I pulled back quickly as she tried to swing her blade and missed—but then she was working on a half-decapitation and to my horror, didn't seem to mind. She screamed again—though with what I didn't want to guess—and pushed the blade straight at me as if she were going to skewer me like a shish kebab. I moved to the right when I believed she was about to strike, certain her momentum would carry her through and past me and I could hack from the back to finish removing her head—but that's not what she did.

Medbh apparently figured out what I was going to do before I did it, so instead of carrying the thrust through, she slowed enough to see which direction I'd go and moved *with* me. She wasn't close enough to actually pierce me so she slashed before she lost her footing. The strike hit my side and the burning agony that came with it knocked the driver right out of the bus. I was alone with no sword; in control and rolling on the ground, bleeding. Curling up in a fetal curl seemed the right thing to do as I lost sensation on that side.

I watched Medbh stomp toward me, dragging her sword on the ground. Mine was gone; back to whatever place the Grimoire pulled it from. She stood over me, her head precariously sitting on her neck. I could see the tear and slice my blade had made at the angle she was standing. I realized she was balancing to keep it on. How could any creature survive that kind of damage? Was she immortal?

"Now my little thing," she said in a scratchy and liquid filled voice. Black blood pooled over the slice and ran down her chest. It also ran out of her mouth as she talked. "Time to find out exactly what you are and why you smell like an Angel *and* a Demon. So let's do a little carving—" she raised her sword up, the pointy end aimed at my chest.

More screams erupted behind me, scaring the shit out of me. I thought she'd already struck and I missed it because I was delirious—until I saw a wolf bound over me and lunge at Medbh, its large jaws opened. Both queen and wolf went backward and I saw something bounce to the side. Guests disappeared into hedges and trees.

"Dags!" Sam's voice was nice to hear as she knelt over me. Her legs and boots were still an odd color of gray but she was moving. if not a bit stiff-legged. Tears streamed down her face. "Oh Lady Darksome, hold still—I can fix it—"

"No," I grabbed her hand when she tried to put it against my wound. "This is really too much this time."

She batted my hand away. "Mike's gone to look for Brendi. We have to get out of here. I don't think it matters anymore if we use magic. So shut up." Sam put her hand on the wound and closed her eyes. The pressure hurt and I closed my own eyes, not to copy her but because it *hurt*. I let out a moan and bunched up my muscles as I felt something creeping along my insides, only it felt as if it were moving from my chest down to my hips. I opened my eyes and saw what looked like ropey, gnarled tree branches wrapping around Sam's arm. Her expression softened and the pain in my side slowly melted away.

I was watching her when she opened her eyes. The branches fell away and she pulled at my t-shirt. "Wow…that's gonna leave a scar."

"I'm really not that worried about it. You know you…Sam?"

But she was already out. Unconscious sitting up. When she started to tip over I scrambled to catch her, feeling only a small twinge where Medbh's sword had hacked a nice hole in me.

The garden was empty and losing its green as I watched. The bushes and trees were now leaf-less and brown. Even the grass died beneath me and turned to dirt. The grand home became a dilapidated husk and the fountain's base cracked, the water gone. But the most disturbing thing was the wolf that'd saved my life was quietly eating Medbh. I could hear it lapping up the blood and swallowing.

I could see the thing that bounced. It was Medbh's head. And it was watching the wolf eat and speaking in my head. *:Now you'll never be able to go back to your world you stupid animal…:*

Medbh's voice was scratchy and no longer filled with gurgling sounds. Mostly because the ground was soaking up her blood. I wasn't even going to argue the fact she was little more than a head with no body. But why make sense now?

The wolf paused and looked over at her and in that instant its outline blurred and folded and turned itself inside out until it wasn't a wolf crouched down with blood on its muzzle, but a girl.

She was nude, with a delicate figure and long red hair. She licked her lips and looked back down at the body before she pushed up on her hands and stood on her feet. She turned toward me and smiled. She couldn't have been more than sixteen…seventeen…and it would have been a very uncomfortable moment with her naked and me clothed, but what really set me back was the black blood on her chin and neck. Evidence the wolf I'd seen was in reality, this young girl.

Or, was the reality the wolf?

"You're Darren," she said in a simple voice and knelt down in front of me. I kept my gaze at eye level and hoped like hell Sam didn't wake up 'cause I was pretty sure she'd call me a pervert and hit me.

I cleared my throat. "Uh…yeah. And you have me at a disadvantage. Have we met?"

She nodded, and then she shook her head.

Well that was confusing.

A noise to my right made me glance over to see Mike move through a line of dead bushes. Puck flew overhead and made *tsk-tsk* noises before he landed on a nearby tree.

Something cold touched my cheek and when I turned back she was in my face. "Your mother talks about you all the time." Her lips met mine. I freaked out for two reasons—one was this was a really *young* girl and I didn't want to have to register as a sex offender and two—I could taste the blood on her lips. I let go of Sam and tried to push this girl off of me as she grabbed my shoulders, straddled me and shoved me to the ground on my back. Let me clarify that I wasn't that weak—she was that strong. Then she shoved her tongue in my mouth, pushing more of that foul blood with it. I wanted to cry out of for help but if I opened my mouth at all I was afraid she would try to push her body inside!

"Brendi!"

Mike's shout and the name he shouted made me freeze. Brendi? Was she nearby and watching this naked girl making out with me? I pushed harder but she grabbed my wrists and shoved my arms back.

She let go and I immediately choked and spit as I tuned on my side. The taste of that stuff was like what I imagined rotten chicken to taste like. I gagged several times and finally managed to get up on my hands and knees.

"What were you doing? What's wrong with you?"

"Daddy!"

Oh. God. No...

My nausea increased when I realized Brendi hadn't been watching. The girl that attacked me...the one that forced the Faerie queen's blood into my mouth...was Brendi.

A FATED FAREWELL

"What the hell were you doing?" Mike said while looking at me.

Eh? I took the edge of my shirtsleeve and rubbed it on my tongue before I answered. Damn! Foul! "Me? I didn't do anything. That girl was the wolf! The one that took off Medbh's head."

"What??"

I pointed to the head. The damn thing was smirking at me.

Mike finally noticed it and took himself and his daughter a good two feet or more away from it.

Medbh laughed. *:Yes…she's never liked me. I took her away from those bullies at school…those mean girls. Gave her the body of a wolf, but did she appreciate it? Nooo…:*

The raspy edge of the voice made my hair stand on end. I sat back on my feet and stared at her. She stared at me. "What did you mean she'd never go back now?"

:It's the rules, boy. As one of my dogs she had the possibility to return to her world. If she could leave my hold. But now that she's tasted my blood, it's the same as tasting Faerie dust.:

I blanched and felt a rush of cold start from my head to my feet. *I* had tasted that blood…Brendi forced me to.

:Yes I see it on your face. You'll be mine too. And then I can finally torture you and see what the hell it is you are.:

"She's…full of it…" Sam said as she rolled over, finally awake. But not up to strength. She was still pale and her face looked sunken. Damn…I hated that I couldn't give back to her all she'd done for me since we met. "The sword couldn't have cut her neck like that unless it was demon made. That means somewhere in you, whether its the book or in your DNA, you're demon. So her blood wouldn't have the same effect on you."

"But what does that mean? And why in the hell did Brendi force it into my mouth?"

Brendi pulled away from her father. "Strength and the ability of control, Darren. Now you have to run…all of you…" She pointed at something past me.

I moved up on my knees. Just over the top of the now dead bushes I could see something toppling the trees, blotting out the sky. It looked like a storm rolling in over the horizon.

A storm traveling a thousand miles an hour. "Mike…"

"I see it."

I got to my feet and helped Sam up on hers. She could stand but she wasn't exactly steady. Mike grabbed some of the skirt off of Medbh's gown and tried to wrap it around Brendi. But she pushed at it and shook her head. "There's no time. You have to take her head back to our world. The only way to do that is to have Faerie blood," she looked at me. "And you're the only one that could change that blood so that it wouldn't keep you here."

"Did you know we were coming, Brendi?"

"Yes. Hob told me."

"He knew you were here."

"Yes. Medbh knows he's rewritten the magic for the Cairn to carry you back to our world unhindered. He's done you a great favor and made a grave mistake. What you see coming knows Medbh's power just collapsed. They'll fight to gain control and they'll scramble to get through all of Medbh's Cairns. They see a chance to take all of you and ride you back. They're going to destroy everything. The only way to stop them is for the three of you to go back through that Cairn. You have to go now!"

Wind from the coming storm whipped dirt and leaves up and blew it in our faces. I took the ripped cloth from Mike, tossed it over Medbh's head, and wrapped it up tight before I carried it. "We don't know where the Cairn is!"

"Just go back through the door you came through. Take the lines back."

I looked around, as did Mike and Sam. "It's not here anymore."

"It is. It's just not the way you remember it," she pointed to the arch we walked under. "It's straight through there. The door to the left of the gate. The gate structure is there…" Brendi looked back at the approaching storm. "You've got to go now!"

"But you're coming with us! You have to come home!" Mike reached out to her.

Brendi took a step back. "I can't, Daddy. I let her touch me with the dust when I thought she was going to let Mommy go. But she lied to me." Tears sprang to her eyes. "I have to stay here. I tasted her blood so she wouldn't have power over me, but I could have dominion over myself." She took several steps back, her hair blown about by the wind. "I love you, Daddy!"

And just like that, she was a wolf again. She turned and bounded in the direction of the ruined home.

Mike started after her but Sam grabbed his arm. "No Mike! We have to get out of here. Dags has the bitch's head—let's put her in the sunlight and see what happens."

I liked that idea, and once everyone was running in the right direction, I took off as well.

As I ran, I had that feeling I always got when I watched a scary movie. That I wasn't alone and something was watching me. Behind me. I didn't want to look back because I was afraid I'd see it was gaining on me. Something struck Mike first. It grabbed at his shoulders and picked him up in mid run. All I could make out were talons, wings and a snake-like body. I reached out with my right hand as Mike's feet passed over my head. *"Isatum!"*

The thing burst into flames. Orange, yellow and then ash. Mike landed in a roll ahead of me. As I ran to him something landed on top of *my* shoulders. I fell forward onto my front and Medbh's head bounced and rolled away from my grasp.

Whatever it was raked something sharp down my back. I screamed and tried to turn over to see it. My thoughts bounced around in my head as I tried to concentrate on the book. I wanted to get the sword again. But the book had something else in mind.

Two shots and the pressure holding me down vanished, but the pain only got worse. I felt Mike and Sam's feet vibrate the dirt and dead leaves under me. Mike reached down to help me stand. His shoulders were raw meat. Blood flowed over his chest and back but he was alive. My back tingled again and this time I felt the wings as they emerged. I was relieved they weren't damaged in the attack. They straightened out and flapped quickly as a crack to our left heralded the collapse of the door.

Our line to the Cairn was gone.

"Damn!" Sam put her hands to her head. "Now what do we do?"

As strange as it sounded when I said it, I knew it was true. "I know the way," I grabbed Mike around the waist. "Hold on. Sam, grab the head!"

"Ew?"

"I don't need girly right now. I need that super bitch you keep tucked in there."

She grabbed the head and then ran at me. The second she was in my arms I bent down and kicked up as my wings flapped and beat as fast as they could. We were airborne, and once again I wasn't in control. Whatever guided my sword, now guided my flight. Which was fine with me because I was feeling really…really…cold.

We broke out in front of the advancing horde and as the gate to the Cairn became visible my wings gave out. We crash-landed near the tree and bench and I lay on my front, unable to move.

"Dags? Come on we've got to get—" Sam hissed. "What the hell happened to his back? It looks like your shoulders."

"Something got him. Come on." I felt Mike wrap his arms around my stomach and hips as he carried me like a football at his side.

"Mike—put him down! Carrying him is making you bleed!"

"I don't have a choice, Sam. You can't carry him and those things are gaining on us."

All I could see was the grass and Mike's shoes. A pause and then the creak of metal and I felt the difference in the air. It was less hot, less oppressive and it smelled more like rotting plants than rotting meat.

Water from the stream splashed onto my face as Mike crossed it. I didn't appreciate it at first, but it did clear my head and wake me up a little. The pain in my back had moved around and surrounded me like a blanket of *oh fucking god that hurts*. I wasn't thinking and I sure as hell wasn't moving.

Until Mike put me down on a soft bed of flowers. I opened my eyes to see one of them. It was something like a bluebell. All the tiny little flowers turned to look at me. Their petals spread to show me tiny smiling faces. I smiled back. "Cool."

"What the fuck was that thing that landed on him?" Sam asked as I felt her ripping my t-shirt. Damn…and that was my favorite Muse shirt.

From the look of the wounds, it was a harpy.

"Mike!"

I felt a slight vibration under me and assumed Mike had collapsed.

Mike's wound is very similar, but not a harpy.

"A snake thing got Mike. But a real harpy attacked Dags?"

I was trying really hard not to pass out. We still had to get home, and I was not going to let Sam do anymore healing on me. Thunder interrupted and all movement over me stopped. I wanted to ask what was happening, but I just couldn't find the energy.

"Hob? What is it?"

You have Medbh's head. Now he really sounded surprised. *You…you cannot stay here. You have to leave now.*

"Dags and Mike can't travel like this…and what'll happen when we get back home? You said we'd go the time and day we came in?"

Only if you use the pool…I am not sure of the time…

There was a long, scary, pregnant pause.

"Hob," Mike said. He sounded like he was in a lot of pain. Thunder cracked the air again. The ground vibrated beneath me and the little blue bells closed their leaves and trembled. "What's…wrong?"

Something was coming.

"What are you not telling us?" Sam demanded. "Hob?"

I do not know about the snake creature and since Mike is moving and speaking, I do not believe they are related. A harpy's talon secretes a poison that paralyzes its prey. Has the Guardian said anything or moved since it happened?

Another pause. I assumed Sam was shaking her head.

Then it is working its way into his bloodstream. The pool…contains a natural healing property. It was the magic I intended to use to make sure you were not made ill on your return to your world. If you take him through, I fear the pool will dry up trying to cure him. If you place Mike in the pool, there may not be enough power to heal Dags, or if you place him in first—

"Then there won't be a way for us to return without consequences," Sam finished.

Put Mike in the pool! I screamed at them. Or I thought I did. The truth? I wasn't doing anything but staring at a shivering blue bell. Hell, I wasn't even sure if I really said "cool" earlier.

Where is your daughter?

Mike sighed. "She's staying. She…ate some of Medbh's body."

Another pause. I hated the pause when I couldn't move and see the conversation.

She consumed the blood?

"So did Dags. She forced him to take some of it."

He has Medbh's blood in him? Hob sounded excited.

Thunder interrupted again. This time it was much louder and I swore I heard the baying of dogs.

"Yeah…is that good?"

Yes it is! Sam, put your magic to use with Mike.

Again there was a pause and I drifted off…only to be jostled awake by Mike reaching under my chest. Apparently Sam worked on him this time.

Please, help me get him halfway into the water. We do not have much time before they arrive. The gate will hold for a short amount of time, but I cannot hold against all of them.

"All of whom?" Sam's voice was loud and clear.

Mike held me across his forearms and then set me into the water. It was cold, damn cold, ice cold on some serious parts of my anatomy. Abruptly, the water warmed and churned just beneath the surface as the water touched my back.

:Hey! I can't see what you're doing!: came the raspy voice of Medbh from my makeshift bag.

That is very disturbing.

Sam laughed. "I'll say…but what's happening? Is Medbh's blood inside of him going to help?"

Dags is both Angel and Demon, fueled by the book in his center. The Grimoire will take that blood and use it to its fullest need. And right now, his need is to heal.

The ground shook and I heard the gate creaking.

"They're here. I thought they couldn't get here," Mike said. "And what exactly are *they*?"

Every denizen of this realm Medbh has ever angered.

:That's a lot of angry,: the bag said.

I knew the moment her head was removed; I just never believed you would bring it here.

"Is that a bad thing? I think Dags figured we would take it to our world and let it burn in the sun."

I hope that is all it will do.

"Are they after her? Those things at the gates? The harpy that attacked Dags?"

Yes. They all want her head so they can torture it through time.

:No one has a sense of humor anymore,: Queen Medbh laughed. Or it sounded like a laugh.

Feeling rushed into my legs as if a dam had been opened. And then the rush spread through my other extremities, and finally my back—and that's where the pain kicked in. "*Aaahhhhh….shit!* Ow…"

Mike was still half holding me in the water. "There we go…back with us?"

"I wasn't gone…just couldn't move. And we need to get out of here…that gate's not going to...shit this hurts…hold all those other assholes," I turned my head to see Hob sitting on the water's edge. "Which is better? To take it with us or leave it here?"

Did you burn her body?

"No. It was mauled a little."

Take it with you. It is best if her head never finds her body. But wrap it in some of the Spiderwyk web. That will keep any of its evil taint from touching the pool's water.

:I ain't got no taint!: Medbh broke out into raspy laughter.

"Can we gag her with it first?" Mike quipped as he helped me crawl out of the pool. I rested on my side, shirtless and shivering from cold as he helped Sam gather up some of the webbing and wrapped the bundle in it. The gate creaked again.

You must hurry.

"Okay how does this work?" They joined me at the edge of the pool, the bundled head in Sam's hands.

You must swim down to the door at the bottom of the pool. It will open for you because you left me a part of yourself. Go through and make sure you close and lock the door on the other side.

"Door at the bottom? Hob, this pool's shallow," Mike said.

Is it?

I watched Mike jumped in first and he disappeared immediately. Sam reached out for Hob's forearm. To my surprise, he took her hand in both of his. "What's going to happen to you? Will they hurt you when they don't find the head?"

I do not know. Do not worry Samantha Hawthorne, Dags McConnell. I have been, and always will be. And if this proves not to be true, then I thank you for not rejecting me, and giving me your time. It is all I have ever wanted.

He pulled her to him and they embraced. When he let go he pushed her into the pool. I nodded to him and started to slide in myself—my back was burning like a son of a bitch—but he grabbed my wrist and held on tight. *Did she grant him the wish?*

I had to think for a second. "No. She didn't." My mind was clear. "Hob…my mother was there. She is there. She was at the party."

Hob looked at me. Or as far as I could tell he looked at me. *I know.*

I searched his featureless face. "You…you knew? You knew my mother was alive and in *Alfheim*? Why didn't you say anything?"

Guardian, you still have a wish you must make. Do not allow anyone else to do so. He moved his hand into mine, shook it as a gentleman, and then shoved me under the water.

KNOWLEDGE iS POWER

Once in the water something grabbed my ankle and pulled me down. Luckily, the water was clear and I could see the hand belonged to Mike. I moved with them and righted myself when he let go. I could see the door below us. It was simple and lay on the pool's floor. The walls of the pool shook and kicked sand up as Sam reached it and yanked it open.

Me, Mike, Sam and a shit load of water were pulled into the hole. The motion made me dizzy as we rode the world's scariest water slide out of the Cairn and into—

The Savannah River.

We came out of a pipe, yelling as we tumbled airborne for a few seconds before we hit the water. It was colder than the water in the Cairn. We broke the surface close to one another and looked around.

"Bonaventure!" Mike pointed to the landmass to my right. The moss-covered oaks were a dead giveaway. That and after we swam with him to the other side, we came ashore below a bench overlooking the river and marsh.

I crawled out and collapsed on the sticky grass. The sun was up and the spring warmth felt good.

"Hey, you guys okay?"

I didn't bother looking up. I figured it was someone in the graveyard that saw us come out.

"Hold on!" Mike answered and I felt him beside me. "Dags, you're still bleeding. In fact…I'm not sure having an open wound in the Savannah River is a good idea."

Like we chose that?

"Dammit…the pool didn't heal him. You're nearly scar-free Mike, but not Dags," Sam put a hand to my forehead. "Oh shit…you're burning up."

I nodded but didn't think much more about it. We were back home. We'd failed to rescue Brendi. But at least we came back with a head. Yippie. "Sam…you might want to hide the head?" I managed to give her this warning before I slipped my eyes shut and checked out for a while, with a burning question forever in my mind.

Was that woman really my mother?

* * *

Mike had been right about the open wounds and the Savannah River water. Not a good combination. I spent a week at Memorial University Medical Center, suffering through a serious staph infection. Sam and Mike stopped by every day, and twice Sam tried to heal it, but she mucked up the machines instead. After that Mike came alone and kept me informed.

The head, when they were able to go back and get it from where they hid it in Bonaventure, had turned to something like porcelain. But Mike said it had the consistency of concrete. It looked like Medbh, painted the way her face had been at the dance. It also talked when you didn't want it to. Sam stuck it in a safe at Mike's townhouse and said she would take it with her when she went back to Louisiana.

Seemed like a good idea to get it away from the Cairn it came through.

And there was the question of Hob. Had he survived? Was he still there? Or had the horde of Medbh's fan club destroyed it all?

"What happened to the mantle?" I asked Mike during one of his visits.

Mike shrugged. He was staring out the window as rain soaked Savannah. "It disappeared, just like Hob said it would."

"I want to go back, Mike. To check on Hob."

"You want to find that woman, Darren."

How was it he always knew what I was really thinking? "I have to try."

"Dags, why would your mother be in *Alfheim*? Why would she have pretended to die in a fire all those years ago?"

"I don't know. I want to ask her those same questions." I toyed with a fold in the starched white sheet. "I saw the locket around her neck. I know it was her."

"Faeries lie."

I looked down at my body and shifted on the bed. "They bite too."

Mike wasn't dealing well with leaving this daughter in *Alfheim*. I was afraid he would do something crazy, like go back there on his own. But he didn't, and I think Sam had a lot to do with that.

Release day came none too soon. The cherry trees were in bloom; the sky was clear and it was a Saturday. The art students were out on River Street, offering up caricatures for sale, personal one of a kind pieces of jewelry and pottery. We'd come straight from the hospital to River Street because I wanted pralines. And I wanted them now.

I hadn't had them until a nurse had given me one. Her mom had bought them for her and she was afraid they'd wreck her figure.

She became my life long friend after I tasted that delicious candy. So I watched them make the stuff on a huge marble slab at River Street Sweets before I bought about ten pounds I was sure would last me a week.

After that we had lunch at Huey's at a table on the patio. I had a muffuletta, Sam got a salad and Mike had red beans and rice, with the promise of sneaking into my room later tonight when the gases were ripe. Yeah…my room. He'd offered me a home there, as long as I got a job and helped pay the mortgage. He was going to have to be in court a few more times, but it looked like the police weren't going to try and pin his daughter's disappearance on him anymore.

Sam was packed and ready to head west. She wanted to wait until she knew I was okay.

I had one question of my own. "So…the last thing Hob told me was you still had a wish." I looked at Mike.

He nodded. "I did."

He and Sam looked away from each other. I frowned. "What happened? Did you try to use it and it didn't work since the mantle was a fake? Wait…where is the mantle?"

"I'm assuming it's still in my closet," Mike said. "I threw it there when I cleaned out my pants pockets. Or it has evaporated by now." He pushed his plate away. He'd eaten every bite of it. The orchestral accompaniment of that many beans would commence as soon as we got back to his place.

I wasn't sure about the looks they were giving each other. I also felt a pang of worry because Thomas and Hob had been adamant about me making the wish, but I'd never shared that with Sam or Mike. And then I had a terrible realization. "Shit…you used it to save me? Guys… it wasn't that bad of an infection—"

"No," Mike shook his head. "That's not what I used it on." He licked his lips.

"Now you're scaring me… did you use it to make Brendi whole again? Is she human and here now?" I looked around, half expecting her to come out and serve us now. Surprise!

"Darren," Sam said and leaned forward. She sat across from me at the table, her expression sincere. "He didn't use it on Brendi. That wasn't possible." She grabbed the check and waved to the waiter. "Let's go."

We walked in silence down the sidewalk to her car. She'd parked it in the lot beside Kevin Barry's Irish Pub. She drove a Jeep Rubicon, silver, with a sleeping wolf resting in the back seat. When Sam opened the back door, Grey bounded out and put her two front paws on my shoulders.

I am very happy to see you, Darren McConnell.

I gave her a hug and she jumped down.

The head is safe in the trunk. It mumbles sometimes but I'm happy to know my jailer is now jailed.

I knelt down beside her. *What about your form?*

I have it back. But I still do not want Sam knowing I am her mother. Will you keep this secret?

"Always," I said aloud.

"Sorry about that—" Sam said before she reached inside the back of the car and pulled a large tan envelope out of the pouch behind the front passenger's seat. "But she seems to adore you," she straightened and handed me the envelope. "I kept it in the car because it's been protected."

I stood and looked at each of them, not sure what wish could possibly be inside of an envelope. When I touched it, a sharp pinprick of a shock ran through my body and I pulled my hand away. "What the…"

Mike took the envelope, took my hand, and put the envelope in it. The shock happened again, and then disappeared. "This was my wish to make, so I asked for a way to return your childhood memories to you."

The sounds of the seagulls, the murmur of people, the water, everything disappeared as I stared into Mike's face. I opened my mouth and then closed it. With trembling hands I carefully tore open the top of the envelope and pulled out a single sheet of parchment paper. To the untrained eye, it was blank on both sides, but to my eye, it was filled with an ancient Babylonian text.

"The spell is older than the book," Sam said. "If you place it into the Grimoire, you'll remember what you've forgotten."

I looked into her face. Though she was smiling at me, I thought I saw a hint of sadness. "What's wrong?"

She looked away from me at the river. One of the large cargo boats was making its way slowly through the water. "When I first touched it, the Mother let me see things. They were some of your memories. And I think I was allowed to see them because you need a warning," Sam looked back at me. "There may be some things you don't want to know."

It took a few seconds before I understood what she meant.

My mom.

"The story my dad and my grandmother told me…the one about me running from the fire and being found in a tree?"

"I can't give you the answers, Dags. You'll have to make the choice to see," Sam put her hand on my forearm. "Mike thought it best to give you the ability and not just make it happen. This way you have a choice. When you're ready."

When I'm ready?

I looked at the page for a few more seconds before I slipped it back into the envelope. When I tilted the envelope I saw transparent images drawn on the surface, much like watermarks on expensive paper. I wiped at my eyes.

Mike put a hand on my shoulder. He stood behind me. Sam pulled me into her arms and I wrapped my arms around her. Mike wrapped his arms around the both of us. He'd given this to me.

He could have wished for so many things, but he'd given it to me.

But Thomas's warning that I should make the wish still rang in my ears. I didn't know why, but holding the page in my hand filled me with a sense of dread.

* * *

After Sam left with promises to keep in touch, Mike and I walked back to his townhouse, cracking jokes about what we'd been through, what we'd seen, and what we hoped to never see again. Once in the kitchen, I put the envelope on the table and he grabbed us a couple of beers.

"You want to come with me to seal the door?" he asked after taking a long swig.

"No…" I did and I didn't. I wasn't sure I could really face the door at that minute and not be overwhelmed with the memories of being attacked. I walked to the window and looked out at the garden. "Actually yeah. I'll come with you."

"You're afraid I'll do something crazy."

"No," I said it almost immediately. "Yes. I can't risk you going all Dirty Harry and going back to *Alfheim*."

We didn't say anything for a while.

"Well," Mike said as he headed to the stairs. "I appreciate the company, and I promise I won't go back."

"Yeah," I called out to him as he climbed the stairs. I drank my beer and stared outside for a very long time.

That night Mike went out with his friend Darius. I begged off, saying I was still tired and needed sleep. But long after they were gone, I searched the kitchen for the largest plastic bag I could find. One that sealed was perfect.

I opened the glass doors, grabbed Mike's box of garden tools, and headed down into the yard. Behind the small fountain were a few large boulders. I picked the largest one and with a quick, "*Elu*," the word for raise up, the boulder levitated a few feet off the ground, high enough for me to dig a deep hole. I dropped the bagged envelope inside and recovered it with dirt.

"*Saplu*." The boulder lowered to the ground. I spent a few more minutes making sure it looked as trim as it had before, then moved to the other boulder to make it look like the one I'd disturbed.

I stood looking at the stone for a long time before I realized I wasn't alone.

To my right sat a wolf. A magnificent white wolf. I took a step back and it whined. A soft, unhappy noise. So I swallowed my nervousness and moved forward again. "Hey...are you a friend of Brendi's? I didn't mean to make you sad."

She—I sensed at that moment it was a female wolf—tilted her head as she watched me. I wiped the dirt off my hand before I offered it to her to sniff, hoping maybe she would let me touch her. I had no idea how she got into Mike's garden.

The wolf stood on all fours and put her paws on my shoulders. I caught the glint of something in her mouth just before she dropped it into my hand. She went back on all fours and then sat looking up at me.

I stared at the necklace and locket. A red stone, a moon and a wolf. It was the same one I'd seen around the neck of the Faerie that knew my name.

When I looked at the wolf I knew it was her. She pushed my hand with her nose. I could just see details of the locket under the light of the porch. It opened—

Emotion overwhelmed me as I looked down at the picture of me... and my mother. The darkness of my past had blotted out the picture, but not it came back to me in brilliant color. It was the same woman.

This time when I looked at the wolf she was no longer a wolf, but the woman in the queen's garden looking at me face to face. We were the same height. I opened my mouth to say something, but she put a finger over my lips. I felt flesh instead of a wolf's paw.

"It's not time, my son. My home is in turmoil—but this could be a gracious step forward. All the answers you need will be given to you. All you have to do is make the wish Hob and Thomas told you to make." Her gray eyes searched mine as she moved her finger from my lips and pulled me to her.

"But they didn't tell me what to wish—just that I had to make the wish myself."

"Yes. You have to make it. No one else can. Do you understand?"

I hesitated. She didn't know Mike had already made that wish for me. She didn't sense the answers buried under the stone in the garden beside us. "Yes but—"

My breath caught when I felt her cold body against my own. The smell of rue and lavender, the scents of my childhood, returned as I wrapped my arms around her and squeezed her tight. "Mom."

"My sweet, sweet boy," she said before she gently pushed me from her but kept her cold hands in mine. "I have to go…"

"Wait. Tell me what you are. Are you Faerie? Are you human? What does that make me? Am I only half human?"

"Sshh," she squeezed my hand. "You are human. I wanted you to be, and I worked hard to make you into what your father wanted. But I can see the scars of his displeasure on your soul."

"His what?" I didn't understand any of this. "My dad's never said more than three words to me. After he said you died, I spent years in boarding schools."

She looked sad. "Make the wish, Darren. Remember everything that happened to you. Now," she kissed the backs of my hands and released them. "I have to go."

I looked down at her feet. "You're standing on the ground. I thought Faeries couldn't touch the ground or they turn to ash."

"I'm not a full blood," she turned to go.

"Mom—what happens if someone else makes the wish?"

"Then you lose the one chance to know who and what you are."

"And if someone makes the wish…for me?"

The look on her face terrified me as she moved with the speed of the wind back to me. She pressed against me and put her hands on my shoulders. "No one else can do that. Do you hear me, Darren? If someone else asks for your memories back—" but she didn't answer. She stopped, smiled and kissed my forehead. "I'm proud of you, Darren. I love you."

And then she was gone. My eyes burned as I called out to her. I ran through the back gate to the sidewalk, turning to the left and then the right to find any sign of her.

After a while, I put the locket around my neck, cleaned the tools, replaced them, locked the door and took a long, hot shower.

MiNUTES TO MiDNiGHT ZOMBiES!!!

I never thought or even considered in the slightest that some of that crap I watched on TV or in the movies was real. Take Zombies, for instance. I mean, seriously? The walking dead? Vampires had more of a chance of fitting into the waking, sane world of the mortal, especially if you explained them as demon-possessed humans.

Totally makes sense, right?

But an animated, walking corpse that feeds off of brains? How is it supposed to eat the brains if it's dead and the stomach's not working? And if it's dead, that means the heart isn't working, which also means there's no blood pumping into the brain, and it's not getting oxygen because the lungs aren't working. So it's just not feasible for such a thing to exist.

Right?

"Dags! Stop daydreaming and whammy this thing!"

Whammy? Really?

My name's Darren McConnell, though most people just call me Dags. I can't remember where that nickname came from. Growing up I was just your average run-of-the-mill ghost-sensing human during those awkward, adolescent years when trying to fit in was harder than passing the eighth grade. Either way, I was small, weird, and a bit of a geek, so I spent an inordinate amount of time inside my own locker or the trashcan just outside the gym door.

I grew to about 5'7—missing the magical height of six feet by five inches. That's when I learned height didn't matter when it came to perception. Wouldn't have mattered if I'd grown to be 6'7 because I told everyone I could see things. In elementary school, I told a kid his dad had died and the kid didn't know it yet, so several of his buddies tied me to a tree and gave me a raw razor buzz cut. My head was a chopped up, bloody mess for a while and I spent the rest of that year home schooled. After that, I never told anyone else what I could see and vowed never to cut my hair again. So I sported a ponytail until recently. Felt it was time to start looking professional.

So by the time I got involved with a Ceremonial cult at the age of twenty-four, I was well established as a long-haired hippy freak.

Weird things happened with that cult. Weird things that led me to having a Witch shove a Grimoire into my soul to save my life.

Yes. I have a book in my soul. And not just *any* book. A book of magic spells.

Got that? Good. Because I need to duck now.

The Zombie swung the top half of a concrete tombstone at my head. I crouched down and ducked to avoid having my brains spattered all over a nearby set of ancient headstones. I was sure my blood would add a certain sense of ambience to the graveyard, but I liked having my brain matter *in* my skull.

As I hoped, the force of spinning that hunk of rock around took the creature into a second rotation. I stood up as it moved the stone away from me. There wasn't going to be a lot of time between passes before the thing swung back around at me so trying to pull a spell from the Grimoire wasn't feasible. A sword slicing through its neck, still not enough time to use.

So…the third option I had was to attempt to *whammy it,* as my best friend wished, with fire.

I moved as far back out of the thing's range as possible. Bonaventure Cemetery was a tight boneyard, speckled with plot-to-plot family gatherings of headstones and mausoleums. Luckily, we weren't in one of the larger plots where massive stone and marble monuments were built to the memory of some patriarch or matriarch of the family. That would have been way too close an area for me. I'm not a big man. I liked open space for that fourth option.

Running.

I turned and faced my opponent as I shouted a single word. *"Isatum!"* It was Sumerian for fire, and boy did it make some fire.

When I first started casting magic, I wasn't sure where the power came from. I assume the Grimoire worked as the catalyst and my own energy, chi, ka, whatever you want to call it, fueled the spell.

Of course, I could be uber wrong.

Fire engulfed the rotting corpse with a bit more force than I intended. Tiny pieces of flying concrete stung my face and bare forearms as the headstone exploded. Then silence.

I had my eyes closed. Which of course was a habit I seriously needed to correct. But I didn't want them to get hit with flying Zombie guts.

When I opened them, nothing moved in front of me. Bits and pieces of Zombie embers floated in the sky like sick little fireflies. I heard a brushing noise just before something clamped down on my ankle like a vise. I looked down to see the bony hand of a torso-only Zombie holding onto me for all it was worth. I screamed like a little girl and hopped around on my non-Zombie-grasped foot while I tried knocking the hand and lower arm off of the other.

A hand grabbed my upper arm. "Hold still."

That was Mike Ross. My oldest friend. My best friend. One of his Desert Eagles gleamed in the moonlight as he pointed it at my ankle.

My eyes bugged. "Not the ankle, not the ankle!"

He fired, and the ugly piece of Zombie flew against a nearby headstone. Bits of flesh, bone and goo splattered on the concrete. A closer look showed that most of the exploded Zombie covered the nearby azaleas and trees. I don't know why I yelled. Mike never missed what he aimed at, and barely missed what he didn't.

Mike looked around the cemetery, the weapon pointed skyward with a bit of wispy smoke curling up from the barrel for effect. Dude was ultra cool. Tall, well-muscled and rugged. Women always saw him first.

Well, he was a good foot taller than me, so *everyone* saw him first.

His body was tense. Mike either sensed other Zombies in the cemetery or he was looking out for us. Either way, I propped myself against one of the adjacent headstones and took a look at my ankle. Other than some seriously gross body fluids smeared over my boots, it felt okay.

Instant, burning pain sliced through my calf on the other leg. I looked down to see a Zombie sinking its teeth into my flesh *through* my jeans. Its remaining arm and hand grabbed at the ankle below it and pulled. Hard. I lost my seat on the headstone and slipped down onto my ass, the back of my head connecting painfully with the concrete.

"Sonofa —there's another one!" Mike shouted.

Ya think? Mike's discovery did not give me comfort because he wasn't aiming at the one biting me. And it also meant he was distracted with his back to me as the Zombie started dragging me away from him.

My vision started to darken, so I shook my head in an attempt to refocus on what was happening to me. A Zombie had its teeth in my calf, a hand on my ankle, and was dragging me with it at a pretty damn good clip away from where we'd been. I tried to see how it was doing this, given that it had its mouth around my muscle and flesh. It was moving backwards—which meant the Zombie was moving backwards while dragging me along on my back. How was that possible?

"Dags!"

Mike's voice was somewhere over my head, meaning he finally noticed I wasn't with him anymore. He was coming up behind me as I traveled. I tried grabbing at anything I could as I passed it. A different headstone, a bush, a piece of statuary. Unfortunately, the same things I tried to grab hold of also worked as instruments of blindsiding. After the third stone knocked painfully into my right elbow, I gritted my teeth and kept my hands inside the ride. This gave me a more than disgusting look at the muncher on my leg. I realized immediately—from what I could see between crashing into obstacles—that this Zombie was less decayed with more meat on his frame. What I initially believed was a one-armed Zombie was actually a two-armed Zombie.

As it tried to grab my other leg, I started stomping at its head in mid cruise.

"Dags—you need to smite it!"

Smite it? Good god, who gave that man a dictionary?

One problem I'd come across when using the fire spell I'd received from the Grimoire was that it drained my energy. One or two big blasts and I was ready for a nap. Anything more than that I was out cold. I had maybe one good blast left in the arsenal and I intended on keeping it handy.

So smiting was out. But chopping was a good secondary. On command, a huge sword formed in my outstretched right hand. I instantly put my other hand on the hilt—it wasn't a lightweight sword—and started hacking at the thing's head. I had to be careful for two reasons: one I didn't want to hack my own leg—it already had a bite in it that was stinging to high hell—and two, I didn't want the sword knocked out of my hands by passing obstacles.

Luckily, I wasn't clobbered by either as I successfully lopped off the thing's arms. Somewhere in there we stopped moving, and I continued rolling to my right. I didn't lose hold of the sword, but I did connect pretty hard with the side of a mausoleum. Those things are made of marble.

Ouchmotherfucker.

No stars this time, just the fringe of an inky blackness closing in from all sides. I could feel what was left of the bastard chewing on my muscle.

That is not a sound I recommend anyone ever have burned onto the hard drive of their brain. The sound of being chewed…on…

I managed to lift the sword and saw the head moving up and down just past my chest. I hacked at it again, but nothing was working. My position was too awkward. It was time for that second smiting. The sword vanished and I held out my hand. *"Isatum!"*

Fire flared from my palm and incinerated the Zombie where it was. Within seconds it was gone. This was nothing like the floating embers from my fire before—this was vaporization Sci-Fi style. It was also an exhausting exercise and I laid on my back, panting, my eyelids heavy.

The pain of the bite didn't disappear with the blast. I lay somewhere behind a huge marble structure with a bleeding Zombie bite on my leg. My head hurt and I wanted to throw up. I wasn't even sure if Mike knew where I was or had seen where I'd been dragged.

This was really bad.

"Mi-Mike," I called out, but I wasn't sure if I used my outside voice or not. My ears felt stuffed with cotton. I recognized the signs of shock—and I was heading down that road. The bite was going to be bad enough—I mean, it was a ZOMBIE bite, for crying out loud. Mike was going to have to kill me now. If we pile on the fact I used magic spells twice and summoned what I called my Guardian Sword…

I was heading toward the great Land of La-La and not expecting to wake up.

Something brushed against my neck, but I wasn't able to move. My eyes were closed, and a weight settled on top of me. "Mike…" I whispered. "It bit me…gonna have to kill me…"

Soft laughter stayed my dive into oblivion for a few seconds as I felt knuckles brush against my cheek, and then a cool hand covered my eyes. "No…not tonight. That's not something I can allow." The voice was female and the accent nice and sexy, but not something I recognized.

The hand on my cheek moved my head to the left and I felt lips brush my neck. "Sshh…just relax, Guardian. It's not your time to die. I haven't even started with you yet."

I felt a sharp pain where she kissed me, and then nothing.

To be continued in MINUTES TO MIDNIGHT, Book II.

Glossary

I am not an expert in the Sumerian language but I am fascinated by it. The following list explains the meanings as the words are used in the book.

Isatum - Fire
Batiltu - Stop
Elu - to lift up
Saplu - to put down
Sihirtu - All
Ati me peta babka! - Gatekeeper, open your gate for me!

Author

Phaedra Weldon is a writer and mother of one. Born in Pensacola, Florida, Phaedra was raised in the lush, green southern tropic of Georgia. She grew up on southern ghost stories told while eating marshmallows around campfires, or on the back of pick-up trucks in the middle of cornfields on chilly October nights. Phaedra currently lives in the South with her daughter.

www.ingramcontent.com/pod-product-compliance
Lightning Source LLC
LaVergne TN
LVHW051000080826
845145LV00009B/2380

* 9 7 8 0 6 1 5 8 1 5 8 4 8 *